T0082761

SHADOWS AND PRETTY THINGS

Emily Blokzyl

SHADOWS AND PRETTY THINGS

iUniverse books may be ordered through booksellers or by contacting:

iUniverse
1663 Liberty Drive
Bloomington, IN 47403
www.iuniverse.com
844-349-9409

ISBN: 978-1-6632-0546-9 (sc)
ISBN: 978-1-6632-0547-6 (e)

Library of Congress Control Number: 2020913086

Print information available on the last page.

iUniverse rev. date: 08/14/2020

To my husband, Michel, who helped me develop
this story from a vague idea to a finished reality:
ILYM.
I won.

CHAPTER 1

At 4:20 am on Sunday, March 4th, in the small Oregon coastal town of Blue Whale Cove, Mrs. Suzy Busterson awoke to her alarm, just as she did at that time every morning. The 49 year-old dressed quickly in long yoga pants, a long-sleeve cotton top and cotton crew socks. She pushed her feet into her soft slippers and padded quietly into her kitchen, turned on the small light beneath the microwave, and hummed "Staying Alive" as she sipped precisely ¼ cup of the protein shake she had prepared the evening before.

Five minutes later, Suzy turned off the small light beneath the microwave. She retrieved her jogging shoes from her hall closet, sat on the small bench in the entryway, slipped off her slippers and put her shoes on, tying them snugly but not tightly.

Suzy moved quietly across her living room and stepped out the back door of her beachfront home and onto her wide deck. And just as she did every morning, Suzy left the door unlocked, because the keys didn't fit comfortably into her outfit.

A few moments later, Suzy's jogging-shoe-clad feet hit the soft sand of the beach and she turned north, breaking into a jog, disappearing into the misty shadows that stretched out along the coast.

Not long after Suzy had faded into the darkness along the beach, the landscape lighting around Suzy's home turned off, temporarily darkening the area in advance of the rising sun.

Immediately after the landscape lighting turned off, a dark shadow crossed Suzy's deck, opened the unlocked rear door, and stepped inside. Precisely two minutes later, the rear door opened and the shadow stepped back out onto the deck, crossed to the bushes lining the edge of the property, and disappeared.

Just after 5:30 am, Suzy stepped off the beach and onto her deck, kicked off her sandy jogging shoes, and stepped into her house. She walked into her kitchen, turned on the small light beneath the microwave, and slowly slipped the remainder of her protein shake while humming "Time to Say Goodbye."

Suzy rinsed out her glass and placed it in the top rack of her dishwasher, then turned off the small light beneath her microwave and moved to the hallway leading to her bedroom, slipping on her slippers as she passed by her entryway bench. It was precisely thirty-four steps and she counted every one of them, more out of habit than desire. But this morning, when she was halfway down the hallway, on step number eighteen, something crunched under Suzy's right foot. She stopped, lifted her foot, and saw the remains of a delicate crystal vase that had been shattered on her hallway floor.

Suzy turned to the beautiful mahogany china cabinet that stood proudly in her hallway, and she immediately noticed the large empty space on the top shelf. The shards of vase on her hallway floor accounted for half this space. A clear acrylic display stand that now lay flat on its back accounted for the other half.

The first anniversary gift that Suzy had received from her loving husband, a beautiful turquoise Fabergé egg pendant, was missing from its usual place on the display stand.

CHAPTER 2

Elnora Landlin stepped around a large mud puddle and came to a stop on the side of the trail, just before an incline. Despite her best efforts to avoid the thorough coating of mud all along the trail, her shoes were still caked with several layers of the sticky substance. She kicked a nearby tree stump with first one shoe, then another, and succeeded in dislodging what appeared to be at least three inches of mud. Satisfied that this was good enough for now, Elnora dropped her shoulder, pulling off the strap of her backpack and sliding it around to her front. She removed a chilled bottle of water, pushed her long brown hair out of her face, unscrewed the cap and took a long drink.

At thirty years old and carrying one hundred twenty pounds on her five foot, nine inch frame, Elnora considered herself fit, but not athletic. She walked every day, usually along the wide beach of Blue Whale Cove, and every Sunday she drove twenty-four miles south to Cape Lookout and hiked all the way out to the point. Walking and hiking provided Elnora with the perfect opportunity to think. She thought about her life and her goals, both those she had already achieved and those she still hoped to achieve, she thought about the book she was reading or the movie she had recently watched, she thought about what she would cook for dinner or how she wanted to rearrange the furniture in her living room, and most of all, she thought about her kids.

Elnora was a second grade teacher at Blue Whale Cove Elementary, and she absolutely loved her job and her students. Every day was an exciting challenge, and every day she prided herself on helping her students improve in some aspect of their life--whether it was academically or socially. That said, while Elnora was in her classroom and juggling all the details that went into keeping twenty 7-year-olds busy, engaged and learning, she rarely had the time to think about what may help the student who refused to continue reading because her friends were all way ahead of her. Or what she could do to help bolster the backbone of the student who crawled under the train table in the corner and cried every time he got something wrong. Elnora loved solving puzzles and challenges, but it was while she was walking or hiking that she had her most brilliant ideas. Like placing her reluctant reader on a different series of books--ones her classmates had never read--so there was no determinable "ahead" or "behind." Or having her sensitive student work with younger students, putting him in a position to correct others so he could see it wasn't a bad thing. Elnora's ideas often worked well, and her students thrived. It was for this reason that Elnora's lifelong friend Chrissy, who was also a second grade teacher at Blue Whale Cove Elementary, always shared information about her most challenging students with Elnora. In many cases, Elnora came up with brilliant solutions for Chrissy's students, too.

Today, Elnora was thinking about a student who was incredibly intelligent--he completed all of his work in about half the time it took most other students to complete it; he could even easily work his way through the third grade work she presented him with--but he was considerably behind on his social development because he was painfully shy. All the other students in Elnora's class loved earning free time so they could play games with their peers and they couldn't wait for the two recess slots each day. Russell, however, clearly dreaded these opportunities, and always carried a book everywhere he went so that he could read rather than socialize. He was a very sweet boy, and Elnora was reluctant to do anything that would restrict his reading, but she also knew that he had to develop socially in order to thrive in school and in life. Even as she stared around at the quiet forest surrounding her, Elnora suddenly had an idea. Russell could help out in the kindergarten, reading to the younger children, and as he became comfortable with that, he could move up to 1st grade to help out and then eventually to his peers in 2nd grade. Elnora smiled at the thought of her gentle giant working with rambunctious little kindergartners, but she also knew that she would have to try it before congratulating herself on her grand idea, because it may not work as well as she wanted. It all depended on Russell.

Elnora took another big gulp of water, screwed the cap back onto the bottle, and replaced the bottle in her backpack. She took a deep breath and looked around at the tall cedars that surrounded her, and the maidenhair and sword ferns that carpeted the forest floor. The trail wasn't entirely deserted--Elnora had passed at least five hikers working their way back to the parking lot and two others on their way out to the point--but it was fairly quiet, which was exactly the way she liked it. She took an even deeper breath, pulling in fresh air that was loaded with the smell of cedar trees and salt water. Beyond the sound of the breeze rustling through the evergreens all around her, Elnora could hear the ocean waves crashing against distant cliffs. She took a shorter, sighing breath, pulled her backpack back on, glanced up at the incline before her, and began to climb.

The incline was steep enough that rainwater had run down off it, making it the driest part of the trail. On the other hand, as the rainwater had run down the trail, it had washed away enough dirt to reveal an intricate maze of tree roots and rocks that hikers had to navigate. Elnora's calves burned as she walked on her tiptoes up much of the incline, and she reminded herself to breathe deeply from low in her stomach rather than pant shallowly from her chest. As she finally crested the top and walked down the slight descent that followed, she continued to maintain her deep breathing and forced herself to keep walking, instead of stopping and sitting on the tree stump at the side of the trail like she sometimes did. She pushed on, navigating her way around the mud puddles that dominated the trail. She greeted the short sections of wooden boardwalk with great relief, as they provided an easy way for her to avoid the absolute worst of the mud. Even though it was slow going and it would certainly require a rather thorough cleaning of her hiking shoes when she returned home, the hike through the beautiful temperate rainforest and the incredible views it provided were well worth it.

The trail curved to the right and as Elnora came around the bend her breath caught in her throat, just as it always did. The trees and bushes surrounding the southern side of the trail had dropped away, revealing a sheer, four hundred foot drop to the Pacific Ocean. The view revealed the long beach that ran south all the way to Pacific City. Haystack Rock stood proudly offshore in the distance, looking impossibly small from so far away. The sound of dune buggy engines carried up to her from just west of the beach, and she smiled, turning to face the open ocean. The sun's reflection on the water created a blinding glare that was both stunning and impossible to look at. Elnora stood still and drank it in, enjoying the warmth. Movement in the water several hundred yards from the shore hinted at the possibility of a small pod of whales--and even as Elnora stared, a tail fluke broke the surface of the water. Elnora gave a poorly-suppressed squeal of delight and bounced lightly on her feet.

Several hikers came up behind Elnora and paused, almost imperceptibly, trying not to be obvious as they stared at the young woman bouncing up and down on her heels in the middle of the trail. Elnora turned to them, her broad smile lighting her face, and said, "There's a pod of whales, there," pointing out into the water. The hikers' faces shifted into looks of comprehension and understanding and they moved closer to the southern side of the trail, looking out where Elnora was pointing. Their cries of delight matched Elnora's own emotions as multiple whale spouts confirmed the presence of a small pod. Cape Lookout was the perfect place to spot whales, seeing as how the two-mile-long peninsula placed hikers incredibly close to the whales' migration path, and Elnora had become accustomed to seeing whales just about every time she made this hike. However, the sight never grew old; her reaction each time was much as it had been the very first time.

After a few more minutes enjoying the sight of the whale pod, and a good length of time after the group of hikers had left her and moved on to the point, Elnora also continued on her way out to the point. The view remained open to the south, and Elnora kept her eyes on the pod of whales even as she stayed to the far right of the trail, well away from the sheer cliff. Elnora was only mildly surprised to discover that the viewing area at the very far end of the point was considerably more packed than the trail had been. There was a small bench that faced directly west toward the open ocean and arguably the best view, and today it held three young children--all under the age of five--who each had a small bag of Cheetos and were each happily, and quietly, snacking away, their fingers and faces growing more and more orange with each passing moment. Standing to the side of the children was undoubtedly their large, extended family, a group of no less than fifteen adults spanning three generations. Elnora quietly applauded them for making the hike together with three young children. She herself would be terrified to bring young children on this hike--the very views that struck her with awe every time she saw them came with such sudden and dramatic drop offs that she could strap the children to her own body and still fear for their safety. Chrissy often teased her about her tendency to over-protect her students whenever they went on fieldtrips. Chrissy herself suffered from severe anxiety--she had since they were children--and it seemed to make her feel better when she could accuse her friend of suffering from the same condition. Elnora didn't mind, especially because she didn't feel anxious so much as prudent and cautious.

There were several other, smaller hiking groups scattered around the viewing area. Most were taking photos or selfies, but some were simply drinking in the view, as Elnora herself loved to do. Elnora moved closer to the very western tip of the point, gazing out into the open water and breathing deeply. There was a very small, very rickety, makeshift fence blocking the end of the point, and while some individuals felt perfectly comfortable leaning over this fence, Elnora preferred to stand a few feet back from it. Again, it was not because she was anxious, she always told herself, she was just prudent and cautious. Not to mention a good example for the young children on the bench behind her.

Elnora never stayed too long at the end of the point, even when the weather was perfect and the view at its very best, as it was today. It was more than two miles back to her car, and she was hoping to make it to the Blue Whale Cove Cafe for lunch in just around two hours. She slid her backpack around to her front, took out her still cold bottle of water, took a long drink, replaced it in her backpack and positioned her backpack comfortably on her back again, took one last good look at the views to the north, west and south, and retraced her steps eastward on the trail. As she passed, Elnora smiled and winked at the children sitting on the bench--a cartoonish rim of orange around each of their mouths now.

A little more than an hour after she had left the far end of the point, Elnora rounded a curve and saw the relatively straight stretch of trail leading up to the parking lot. Just ahead, the trail that led down to the beach broke off to her right. She had taken that trail once and it was definitely beautiful in its own right, but the hike back up the side of the mountain was intense and the views were just not to the same spectacular level as the views on the Cape Lookout trail, so she stuck to the main point trail every week now. There was also a trail that led to the north, but she had heard that it was very boring and almost viewless, so she had never taken that trail. Part of her was curious, and she thought that someday she may take the trail just to see where it led, but the other part of her felt that if what she had heard was true, she would wind up feeling like she'd wasted her energy on a dissatisfying hike.

Elnora's calves were aching from the long, steadily uphill hike, but she relished the sensation and pushed herself to move a little faster over the last few steps. The final part of the trail inclined steeply upward, and Elnora was panting by the time she reached the edge of the parking lot. Along with her Honda Civic, there were about ten other cars in the lot, but only one other person. He was leaning into the backseat of a car that had most certainly seen better days--a lot of them. The paint had long since faded and eroded away, leaving a matte gray color that was less than flattering. Elnora ventured a guess that the car was nearly as old as she was, and she assumed it must be a Subaru or Toyota--those cars always seemed to last forever.

The man leaning into the car was wearing thick black hiking boots, worn jeans and a red-and-black checked, long-sleeved flannel shirt. When he came out of the backseat of his car, Elnora noticed that he was about her age--maybe just a few years older. He had short, dark brown hair and a very handsome face. He must have felt her staring at him because he turned and looked right at her. Elnora immediately turned away, closing the remaining distance to her car and pressing a button on her fob to unlock the doors. She threw her backpack across the driver's seat and onto the passenger seat and then got in, closing and locking the door behind her.

Elnora started the engine of her car but didn't drive away immediately. Instead, she removed her not-quite-cold bottle of water from her backpack and took another drink, keeping an eye on the man behind her in her rearview mirror. He pulled a very large backpack out of the back of his car, closed the door and locked the car, adjusted the backpack on his back, and headed off toward the point hiking trail. Elnora smiled--he looked like he was going on a week-long backpacking trip. He stepped onto the trail and sank down out of sight as he descended. Elnora put her car into reverse, backed up out of the parking spot, put her car into drive, gave the beat-up car--she was fairly certain it was an old Toyota station wagon--one final glance, and drove out of the parking lot, turning north toward Blue Whale Cove.

CHAPTER 3

Elnora had grown up and lived her entire life in Blue Whale Cove, a small coastal town of 5,437 people (soon to be 5,438 people when Misty Gunders had her baby). Her parents had met while working together in a large commercial bank in downtown Portland, and one of the many dreams they shared was their burning desire to get away from the busy, crowded city and live someplace where they could have space and plenty of fresh air. Living in Blue Whale Cove meant a one and a half hour commute each way to work, but they had never regretted it. They still lived in Blue Whale Cove, in the same house that Elnora had grown up in, but now they traveled often, both for work and for pleasure, and Elnora saw them every six to eight weeks.

Throughout Elnora's adolescence, teenage and young adult years, she had traveled with her parents all around the country, exploring new towns, cities and places. She enjoyed the sunny warmth of southern California, the excitement of

Times Square in New York City, the beautiful colors in New England during the fall and the jaw-dropping landforms scattered throughout the Southwest, but she was always happy--even relieved--to return home to Blue Whale Cove. She lived for four years in Corvallis, earning her bachelor's degree in teaching at Oregon State University, before happily returning home and securing a job at Blue Whale Cove Elementary the moment she applied.

Blue Whale Cove covered two and a half square miles in a narrow rectangle that hugged the coast. Hwy 101 was Blue Whale Cove's Main Street, and travelers passing through the town saw the majority of commercial properties the town had to offer in a short half-mile stretch. Blue Whale Cove gas was southernmost, a two-pump service station that had been in the same family since opening in 1923. It was followed by Blue Whale Cove Gifts, Blue Whale Cove Trinkets, Blue Whale Cove Treasures, and Blue Whale Cove Secrets, a set of family-owned boutiques and novelty gift shops that turned a decent profit with tourists. Rather than openly competing with one another for business, the boutique and gift shop owners had a friendly meeting each week to go over any new products they intended to purchase. The goal was to ensure that nothing found in Blue Whale Cove Gifts, which focused primarily on handmade items, could be found in Blue Whale Cove Trinkets, which focused primarily on useful and decorative kitchen items, or in Blue Whale Cove Treasures, which focused primarily on hand-blown glass items, or in Blue Whale Cove Secrets, which focused primarily on jewelry and watches.

Past Blue Whale Cove Secrets was Blue Whale Cove Coffee, the only dedicated coffee shop in town, and inarguably much, much better than the products provided by any of the big coffee chains that had tried to muscle their way into the town over the years.

After Blue Whale Cove Coffee came Blue Whale Cove Books, a charming, two-story bookstore where readers were encouraged to curl up in one of the many comfy armchairs placed around the shop and read as long as their hearts desired. No one was quite sure how this unique policy contributed to or affected the bookstore's viability, especially since more than a few residents took full advantage and read entire books in the store so they didn't have to purchase them. It was assumed that between tourists making purchases as they passed through town and the owner's family money (of which there was a lot), there was no threat to the bookstore's viability.

Next came the fifty-room Blue Whale Cove Inn and Blue Whale Cove Inn Restaurant, both of which had been in the same family since their joint opening in 1904. The rooms at the inn were simple but clean and cozy, and it was usually never less than half full. In the past there had been some talk about either expanding the inn to handle the busier times of the year or adding another motel in town, but both ideas were shot down as the residents preferred to preserve their small and quaint town. The inn restaurant provided a broad and varied menu that was updated every six months, and the food was well-liked by residents and travelers alike.

Blue Whale Cove Market came next, and while it was not by any means a full-sized grocery store, it carried enough of the basics to help residents who needed to make "a quick stop at the store" and didn't want to have to run all the way down to Tillamook. Unlike many small-town markets, Blue Whale Cove Market didn't take advantage of its monopoly and raise its prices to absolutely unreasonable levels, but rather managed to keep its prices at a more competitive level.

Finally, there was the Blue Whale Cove Cafe, an adorable dive that specialized in comfort food and dishes featuring local, fresh-caught seafood.

North of Blue Whale Cove Cafe the properties turned residential, with beautiful, tasteful beach homes lining both sides of the road for another half a mile--all the way to the town limits.

Running parallel to and just east of Main Street was 2nd Street, where Blue Whale Cove Library and Blue Whale Cove Elementary sat, adjacent to one another. Blue Whale Cove Library housed just over 50,000 books--a decent amount for a town that size--and it was well-used and enjoyed by both town residents and the travelers who happened to stumble upon it during their visits.

Blue Whale Cove Elementary delivered Kindergarten through eighth grade to roughly seven hundred students, while Blue Whale Cove High, situated further northeast, delivered ninth through twelfth grade to roughly five hundred students. There were more residences--many of them beach cottage style and all of them very charming--north and south along 2nd Street, as well as 3rd Street, 4th Street and 5th Street, which was where Elnora lived. The Blue Whale Cove Police Station and Blue Whale Cove Fire Station were on Cedar Street, which bisected Main Street just north of Blue Whale Cove Trinkets and ran straight all the way through to 5th Street. Apart from the main grid of streets in between Main Street and 5th Street, a web of smaller streets curved off to the north, east and south, weaving back through gentle hills. Many of the town's larger and more expensive homes lined Main Street, where they had mostly unobstructed views of the Pacific, but there were quite a few beautiful homes back in the hills as well, where there were larger property parcels. Though Elnora would never deny that some of the best views were on the hilly streets outside of the main grid, she also preferred living closer to "downtown" because it allowed her to walk most places.

The residents of Blue Whale Cove took great pride in maintaining their little town, and there was no building or home that had last been painted more than five years prior. Even when a property owner couldn't handle the painting himself, whether due to physical or financial issues, the town would quickly rally around him and get the job done. Over seventy percent of the properties owned in Blue Whale Cove remained in the same family they had been sold into when they were first built, and it was that exact family longevity that gave the town its friendly, large family feeling, where everyone knew everyone else. This was one of Elnora's favorite things about Blue Whale Cove, and she couldn't imagine putting down roots anywhere else.

Elnora cruised down Main Street as fast as she dared and pulled into a parking spot in front of Blue Whale Cove Cafe just as Jeffrey Menda stepped in front of the glass door and put his hand on the open sign. Jeffrey was the owner of Blue Whale Cove Cafe, and though no one knew exactly how old he was, the general consensus was that he must be in his mid-sixties. He refused to retire, telling everyone that working kept him young and healthy. He had never married, giving his entire heart and soul to the cafe instead, and Elnora couldn't remember a single time when she had come in and he hadn't been there. Jeffrey looked up and caught Elnora's eyes as she put her car in park and shut off the engine. He smiled, shook his head and pushed the door open as Elnora opened her car door.

"One of these days, I'm not going to be here and you're gonna miss Sunday lunch, Elnora," Jeffrey said, flipping the sign so that it read "closed". Elnora smiled.

"I'm lucky to have you, Jeffrey," Elnora jumped up the three steps in front of the cafe, kissed Jeffrey on his wrinkled cheek, and stepped in through the door he held open for her. The cafe was small--the mandated capacity was just thirty people--but as the lunch hour was coming to a close it was nearly deserted, with only three other customers sitting on stools along the counter. Along the front windows of the cafe were a series of booths with bright red, vinyl seats. The walls of the cafe were sparsely decorated with metal road signs that lent just enough ambiance to look cute without cluttering the space.

Elnora slid onto a red vinyl stool in between two other customers, turning to the man on her left. Steve Cartha was seventy-six years old, with just a patch of short gray hair around the crown of his head, but a thick gray beard and mustache. He had worked as a lumberjack, just like his father and grandfather before him, and he and his wife were one of the few first-generation families living in Blue Whale Cove.

"Hello, Steve, how are you today?" Elnora patted the older man gently on the shoulder. Steve put down his roast beef sandwich, turned to her and grinned in between chews, revealing impeccably white dentures.

"Pretty darn good, Elnora. And you?" Steve answered in a raspy voice as soon as he had swallowed.

"I'm well, thank you. And how is Miriam?" Elnora asked. Miriam Cartha was seventy-two years old, and a bit of a hero in Blue Whale Cove. It was because of Miriam that the Blue Whale Cove library was as large as it was today--when she had arrived forty years ago, it had been a mismanaged assortment of roughly fifteen thousand books. She lobbied at Town Hall until they agreed to let her step in as the librarian, with the caveat that she couldn't drain the treasury of funds simply to "fancy up" a library that very few people ever used. Miriam managed to raise the money she needed to perform a thorough renovation of the building and purchase an additional twenty thousand books. Unsurprisingly, the library became very well-used after that point, and the town had organized a permanent library fund that allowed the book collection to steadily grow over the years. Steve nodded toward Elnora, pushing a couple french fries into his mouth.

"She's well. She's started on the spring cleaning and organizing, which is why I'm here," Steve smiled again, grabbed his soda and took a long sip. Elnora nodded, patted Steve gently on the shoulder again, and turned to the man sitting on her right.

Frank Blackson was buried in his book, trying hard to pretend that he was oblivious to everyone around him. Known to all as the resident "grump," the eighty-two year-old was really a kind old man who simply acted as though he preferred to be left alone. Those who knew him well knew exactly how to talk to him, which often involved just acknowledging that he was there and he was important, without bombarding him with too many questions. Frank was a third-generation Blue Whale Cove resident, and he had once been the Blue Whale Cove postmaster.

"And you, Frank? How are you today?" Elnora asked.

"Fine," Frank grunted. A less careful observer would assume that Frank was bothered by the interruption, but Elnora caught the small smile turning up the corners of his mouth.

"Glad to hear it," Elnora responded, smiling gently.

"Okay, what'll it be today?" Jeffrey asked from the other side of the counter, placing a glass of ice water in front of Elnora. Elnora winked at Jeffrey, grabbing her glass and taking a long drink. "The usual it is!" Jeffrey clucked, walking along the counter to the kitchen entrance and disappearing from view.

Elnora grabbed a napkin from the dispenser in front of her and mopped up the small puddle of condensation that had formed on the counter around her glass. Steve turned toward her and asked, "So, have you heard?" Elnora looked at him, a quizzical look on her face.

"Heard what?" Elnora asked.

"You don't know yet!" Steve chuckled, his gentle guffaws starting a mild coughing fit that ended when he took another sip of his soda.

"Know what?" Elnora repeated, her voice calm and patient. If there was one thing that working as a 2nd grade teacher had taught her over the past eight years, it was that patience was most definitely rewarded. Eventually. Next to her, Steve's breathing calmed and he cleared his throat.

"Suzy Busterson was robbed!" Steve sounded delighted, but Elnora knew that it was not the news that delighted him, it was being the first to share the news with someone in this town--that was a rare event indeed.

"What?" Elnora pictured Suzy's house--the largest beach house on the western side of Main Street. At 3,500 square feet, Suzy's house had a lot of extra room that she and her husband didn't really need, especially since he was out of town more than he was at home. It was a long, thin, ranch-style home, stretched along the beach in order to maximize the views from every room and every window. The master suite sat at the southern end of the house, with a long hallway separating it from the entry and main living areas. The three guest bedrooms, office and two additional bathrooms were on the northern end of the house. In the middle of the house, fronted to the west by a wall of windows, there was a beautiful dining area, a large, eat-in kitchen, and a huge living room. In the center of the wall of windows, at the point where the kitchen and the living room met, a set of French doors led out onto a large wooden deck and the beach and ocean beyond. "When?"

"This morning, while Suzy was out for her jog. When she came back she stepped on the broken shards of one of her crystal vases, and that's when she noticed her egg pendant was missing," Steve's voice was cracking with his excitement.

"The Faberge?" Elnora asked, remembering the pendant from the last time she had been at Suzy's house. It had been delicate and beautiful, but something Elnora couldn't imagine ever owning herself. Steve nodded. "Why on earth would someone want to take that?" Elnora asked.

"That's the question everyone is asking," Jeffrey had returned from the kitchen, and he placed Elnora's open-faced tuna melt on the counter in front of her. Elnora watched Steve's face fall with disappointment--he had wanted to tell the whole story. She smiled and squeezed Steve's arm gently, before grabbing her fork and knife and cutting into her sandwich. "Sure, the pendant is nice to look at and it's worth a good amount …"

"$30,000!" Steve interjected.

"But it's not exactly the best item for a thief to nick. It's registered with Faberge and insured to boot, which means it can't be sold on the open market. And if the thief intends to sell it on the black market …"

"Did they take anything else?" Elnora interrupted around a mouthful of gooey cheese, warm tuna and soft bread.

"No, and that's the other thing. If they do intend to sell on the black market, why didn't they take anything else? They were standing right in front of her China cabinet, with all its treasures. He could've made off with over a hundred grand, easy, and it wouldn't have taken him much longer than it did to grab the pendant."

"Well maybe a little longer--you'd have to wrap the

crystal pieces so they wouldn't knock into each other and chip or break," Elnora reasoned.

"But that's not even the weirdest part," Steve said solemnly.

"It's not?" Elnora asked.

"No," Steve said, excitement filtering into his voice once again. "The thief must've come in the back door while Suzy was out running. You know how Suzy leaves the door unlocked, and there was no signs of forced entry anywhere else in the house. So that means, in order to get to the pendant, the thief had to walk by the entryway table." Elnora pictured the layout of Suzy's house, from the back door, through the kitchen and living room area, to the entryway, and then into the hallway, and nodded. "Well that means that the thief walked by three hundred dollars in cash lying openly on the entryway table. Twice!" Steve finished excitedly. Elnora frowned, though Steve didn't see it. Jeffrey caught it and leaned forward.

"Suzy's cleaners come tomorrow. She always sets the money out on the entryway table on Saturday or Sunday morning, so she won't forget," Jeffrey explained.

"Oh. So the thief walked past the money, grabbed the pendant, walked back past the money, and then left?" Elnora clarified as she cut another bite of her sandwich.

"Exactly!" Steve nearly shouted. He seemed to finally notice that he was being a bit too overzealous in a situation that demanded decorum, and he worked hard to calm himself. "It's got Suzy and the police all twisted in knots. Even if you could move the pendant and collect $20,000 or so for it, who would pass up the opportunity to pick up some cash that's just lying there?" Elnora shrugged, taking a sip of water.

"What if the thief couldn't see the money lying on the entryway table? I mean, it's still pretty dark outside between

4:00 and 6:00 am," Elnora reasoned. Out of the corner of her eye, she saw Frank shake his head.

"That porch light she has is as bright as the damn sun, and it shines right through the beveled glass at the top of her front door. Her entryway would've been as brightly lit as if the sun was streaming in," Frank grumbled. "In fact, it was damn bold of the thief to step through the entryway, since they would've been fully illuminated for a few seconds."

"Yeah, but for who to see?" Steve asked. "There's no one directly across the street from Suzy, and no one else is out that early." Frank grunted in response, which was the closest he ever came to admitting someone else had a good point.

"Is Suzy okay?" Elnora asked, picking up the last square of her sandwich and placing it in her mouth. She pushed it into her cheek for a moment to finish her thought, "I mean, is she upset?"

"Well of course she's upset," Steve said, "But mostly because someone was in her house and that makes her feel unsafe. She's not really worried about the money lost in the pendant--her insurance company will surely cover that once they get the police report and carry out their own investigation," Steve's tone indicated that there was no love lost between him and insurance companies, "I suppose she'll start carrying her keys in her jogging outfit now, regardless of what the fashion police would think," he chortled. Frank cleared his throat, which was his way of suppressing a chuckle.

"Chief Hinson says it's the first property crime reported in Blue Whale Cove in over ten years--I think we all have the right to feel a little upset," Jeffrey offered. Elnora nodded. "Suzy says the funny part is that while she loves the egg pendant, she hasn't worn it in twenty years. She isn't even sure that she would've noticed it was missing so soon, if it hadn't been for the broken vase on the floor. The thief must've been spooked when he grabbed the pendant and accidently hit the vase." Steve nodded knowingly.

"That happened to Miriam some ten years ago," he looked up and saw confused looks all around him. "No, she wasn't a thief. I meant she didn't notice that something was missing until it had probably been missing for quite awhile," he explained, and everyone nodded together. "She was doing her annual deep house cleaning and organizing, and when she came to her small jewelry cabinet on the shelf in the bedroom, she accidentally hit it and it fell to the floor. It was only as she picked up the jewelry to put it back in the jewelry box that she noticed that the little ruby ring that had been handed down from her great-grandmother was missing. She couldn't even remember when she'd last seen it. She assumed it would turn up eventually, but to this day it never has. I don't know if she's more bothered by the fact that she's missing a precious family heirloom or by the fact that she's obviously missing some nook or cranny around the house when doing her annual deep cleaning."

"A little of both, I'm sure," Elnora said gently. Steve nodded. Elnora sighed and shrugged her shoulders, "Well I'm glad that Suzy is okay!" The three gentlemen around her all nodded. Elnora slid back off her chair, pulling $20 out of her pocket and placing it on the counter. Jeffrey shook his head and opened his mouth to protest, but Elnora was ready. "Thank you for the delicious sandwich, Jeffrey, as always, and I'll see you guys around!" she turned and quickly made her way over to and out the door, down the steps and to her car. By the time Jeffrey made it around the long counter and over to the door, Elnora had backed out of her parking spot. She glanced up at him, waved, and drove south, towards Cedar Street and home.

CHAPTER 4

Elnora pulled her car into her driveway, put it into park and shut it off. She looked up at her house--a charming beach cottage painted in a soft yellow with decorative white shutters. The landscaping was very minimalistic, consisting of a small patch of grass and a handful of flowering bushes. On the front porch, just to the right of her front door, sat a large, resin elephant holding a "Welcome" sign. Elnora was not a big decorator--in fact the walls of her home were mostly bare--but she loved elephants and couldn't resist this one when she saw him in the Tillamook Fred Meyer Garden Center.

At 900 square feet, Elnora's cottage boasted two small bedrooms, one bathroom, an eat-in kitchen and a living room--all on a square layout. Despite the fact that Elnora could never comfortably hold social gatherings of over two people in her home (not really a problem since there were plenty of friends all through town who had much larger homes and were happy to hold any and all social gatherings there), the cottage was absolutely perfect for her and she loved it dearly.

Elnora stepped out of her car and closed and locked the door. Instead of walking to her front door, however, she turned and headed north on 5th Street. Five minutes and twenty houses later, Elnora walked up the driveway to a small beach cottage that was almost a perfect copy of her own. It too was 900 square feet, with two bedrooms, one bathroom, an eat-in kitchen and a living room on a square layout, but it was painted a soft pink color, with no shutters, and the front yard was a carpet of white stones with a small cedar tree planted in the exact center. To the right of the front door sat a large, resin elephant holding a "Welcome" sign. Chrissy had seen Elnora's elephant and loved it so much that she raced down to the Tillamook Fred Meyer to pick up her own. It always made Elnora smile--it was like the grown-up version of friendship bracelets.

Elnora opened the screen door and knocked gently on Chrissy's front door. It was opened immediately--either Chrissy had just been walking by or she had been sitting on her couch, which was placed against the wall directly adjacent to the front door.

"Hi! Come on in--I just have to finish moving my clothes into the dryer so they don't mildew!" Chrissy puffed and then rushed off to the garage. Elnora shook her head and walked straight back to the bathroom. It was nestled between the two bedrooms--Chrissy's at the back, and the spare at the front. Chrissy's bedroom was much like Elnora's, filled with simple but tasteful furniture consisting of a full-sized bed, a long, seven-drawer dresser and a single bedside table. Several glass jars of shells were placed on the bedside table and the dresser, and the wall above the dresser was adorned with a large painting of the beach. Soft curtains covered the one window, and all the colors were cool and light, perfectly complimenting the cottage.

Elnora didn't know if Chrissy's spare room was at all like her own, because she had never seen it. When Chrissy was ten years old she had received a lockable hope chest. Elnora saw the inside of it once, shortly after Chrissy received it. It was lined with beautiful, fragrant cedar pieces that were deep red with beautiful, natural striations. When she had asked Chrissy about it a few years later, Chrissy confirmed that she liked to keep things in it, but not in the way most people used hope chests. Rather than keeping her most precious treasures in it, Chrissy said she kept the things she was embarrassed about in it. It was her "messy drawer," something she was too embarrassed to show others--even her closest friend. Eventually, Chrissy's "messy drawer" hope chest grew into Chrissy's "messy drawer" hope chest and closet. Then, when she bought this little cottage, Chrissy's "messy drawer" became her entire spare bedroom. Elnora assumed the hope chest was in there, as she didn't see it anywhere else in the house. She had once expressed concern that her friend was becoming a bit of a pack rat, but Chrissy assured her that it wasn't that bad at all--she just appreciated having one space that she didn't have to keep perfectly cleaned and organized or be embarrassed when others saw. She could even work on craft projects and leave an utter mess to clean up later, without anyone ever knowing, and she liked having it that way. Elnora tried to assure her friend that no matter how messy the room was, she would never judge her for it, but Chrissy simply wouldn't budge. She insisted that her "messy drawer"/craft room was cathartic for her, largely because she knew that no one else would ever see it. Elnora let it go at that.

Elnora washed her hands with the seashell-shaped soap in the seashell dish next to the bathroom sink and walked out to the kitchen. The teapot was already on the stove, but when she lifted it, Elnora noticed that it was cold and almost empty. She shook her head again, smiling, and filled the teapot under the faucet before placing it on the stove and turning the stove on. Elnora loved her friend dearly, but there was no arguing that she was incredibly scatter-brained. In class, she had everything planned out perfectly and written down in great detail so that she never forgot anything, and she was a very good teacher as a result. She had never bothered to carry that successful action back to her home, and Elnora had long since become quite used to coming over for Sunday tea only to find that her friend had failed to adequately prepare for tea.

The door from the garage opened and closed and Chrissy appeared in the kitchen a few moments later. Chrissy was slightly shorter and slightly bigger than her friend, standing at five feet eight inches and weighing one hundred thirty pounds, with light brown hair that was cut just below her chin. Like Elnora, she was a second-generation Blue Whale Cove resident, though Chrissy's parents had sold their house and moved to Ashland when Chrissy graduated from high school. They loved Oregon, they told Chrissy, but they wanted to move as far south as possible so that they could enjoy more warm, sunny weather throughout the year. Chrissy didn't mind at all--she enjoyed visiting her parents and taking trips from Ashland down to San Francisco. Chrissy glanced at the stove and saw that the teapot had been filled and put over a lit burner.

"Oh, thank you! I was starting to prepare the tea--I promise I was--and I suddenly remembered the load of clothes I started yesterday. Thankfully they don't seem to have mildewed at all yet, so they should be fine," Chrissy reached into a cabinet and pulled out two matching elephant mugs.

"Did you turn the dryer on?" Elnora teased gently. Chrissy groaned.

"Yes, of course I turned the dryer on!" Chrissy placed the mugs on the small, round kitchen table and then turned and paused, clearly thinking.

"Do you want to go check?" Elnora couldn't suppress the giggle that rose in her chest. Chrissy stomped her foot in mock irritation.

"No, I don't want to go check!" Chrissy turned back to a different cabinet and pulled out her tea caddy, placing it on the table between the mugs.

"Shall I go check?" Elnora offered, her giggle transforming into full-blown laughter now.

"No!" Chrissy asserted. She pointed a finger at Elnora. "You, sit!" she commanded, and then she turned back to the kitchen and pulled the honey pot out of the pantry, before walking over and placing it on the table by the tea caddy. Elnora sank down into her chair slowly, still laughing. Chrissy tried to look irritated but failed miserably, her face breaking into a broad smile as she sat down across from her friend.

"Spoons," Elnora said simply. Chrissy grimaced and stood again, pulling open a drawer and grabbing two spoons before sitting down again. The teapot began to whistle and Chrissy moved to stand again, but Elnora waved her down and went to grab the teapot herself, placing it carefully on a stone trivet on the table. Chrissy waved toward the tea caddy and Elnora opened it, pulling out a thyme tea before pushing the caddy back toward Chrissy. "By the way, I like the new soap dish in the bathroom."

"Thanks! I got it at Treasures yesterday," Chrissy said, selecting a peppermint tea from the caddy before pushing it back to the center of the table.

"It's pretty fancy--you're not worried it'll break?" Elnora asked, unwrapping her tea bag.

"Honestly? Yes," Chrissy admitted. "I really hesitated before buying it," Chrissy shrugged as she unwrapped her tea bag and placed it in her mug, "But it's pretty, and you know how much I love beach things!"

"Yes, you do," Elnora smiled, glancing around at the various, beach-related trinkets that decorated Chrissy's home. Her favorite was a tall blue vase that sat on the windowsill in front of the sink. Chrissy's parents had given it to her for her twenty-fifth birthday, and though it never held flowers as was intended, it was still greatly admired and enjoyed.

"So, how was your hike?" Chrissy asked.

"Muddy, but good," Elnora wrapped the tea bag string around the handle of her mug and then carefully poured in hot water. "There was a pretty big whale pod near the point today. I'm guessing they were either breeding or feeding--they were tightly packed together," she grabbed a spoon and dipped it into the honey pot, turning it over slowly to wrap the honey around the bowl so that it wouldn't drip on the way to the mug. Chrissy mirrored her, stirring honey into her own tea. Elnora lifted her mug, blew on her tea for a few seconds, and then took a microscopic sip of the hot tea. Chrissy preferred to wait, letting her tea cool to nearly room temperature before sipping it.

"Oh--I almost forgot!" Chrissy jumped up from the table and headed back into the kitchen. "Would you like some biscuits?"

Elnora frowned. "Biscuits?"

"Yeah, cookies. The British call them biscuits," Chrissy rifled through a cupboard.

"Are they British cookies?" Elnora asked, taking another tiny sip of hot tea.

"I don't think so," Chrissy said, pulling out a tin container. "Let me see … nope, they're from New Jersey," she brought the container to the table and set it down in front of Elnora.

"Where did you get them from?" Elnora asked, prying open the lid and revealing rows of buttery shortbread cookies. She removed a cookie and bit into it. It was sweet, but not too sweet, and perfectly crunchy.

"From Rain Walken. She took a trip back east with her parents in order to visit family and brought me back some biscuits," Chrissy grabbed a cookie and bit into it. "That's what Rain called them when she gave them to me--I'm just rolling with it," Elnora smiled and nodded, taking another sip of her tea. "They also brought me a throw for my bed and some organic maple syrup. I swear--every time they take a trip, it's like Christmas for me," Chrissy polished off her cookie and grabbed another from the tin. Elnora shrugged.

"They're grateful to you, and they have the means to show it," Elnora took another cookie from the tin and bit into it.

"Hey, I'm not complaining!" Chrissy smiled and leaned back in her chair.

"Me neither," Elnora said, biting into her cookie.

"Pretty good, huh?" Chrissy smiled at her friend, who nodded. "Why do things always taste better when they're brought in from out of town?" Chrissy asked, taking another cookie from the tin.

"Because they're brought in from places that definitely

know what they're doing," Elnora said, taking another bite of cookie and a sip of hot tea.

"How nice to have enough money to buy whatever you want, from wherever you want," Chrissy mused, taking a small nibble of her cookie.

"Absolutely," Elnora agreed. "Speaking of the financially fortunate, did you hear that Suzy Busterson was robbed?" Elnora asked. Chrissy's countenance paled and she leaned forward onto the table.

"What?" Chrissy breathed. Elnora reached forward and placed her hand on her friend's arm.

"It's okay, Chrissy," Elnora soothed. "Suzy was out for her morning jog, she wasn't hurt." Chrissy's breathing came in short puffs.

"I think I'm having an anxiety attack," Chrissy groaned, putting a hand to her forehead. Elnora squeezed her arm.

"Just breathe, deeply and slowly. It has nothing to do with you--Suzy has a big, fancy house on the beach with some fancy, expensive items. She also likes to leave her home unlocked for an hour every morning and everyone in town knows it. It's an unfortunate truth that it was likely just a matter of time before someone took advantage. You, on the other hand, have a small, quaint cottage tucked back in the town that is always locked tight. And I'm quite certain a thief would allow you to keep your biscuits and shells," Elnora waved around at the small, ornamental vases of shells set on Chrissy's windowsills and shelves. Chrissy forced a smile and nodded, her breathing slowing to normal.

"I just..." Chrissy began, and then swallowed, looking up at Elnora with large, fearful eyes.

"I know," Elnora interrupted. "You don't like bad things happening to good people. But I assure you, Suzy is totally fine. And you will be too--guaranteed," Elnora smiled at her friend. Chrissy returned a shaky smile.

"I'm glad she's okay," Chrissy managed, "And not too upset."

"Well I think her insurance will cover her loss, so that helps quite a bit," Elnora took another sip of her tea and looked again at her friend, who was beginning to look better.

"That's good," Chrissy nodded, trying a small sip of her own tea. It was still a little hotter than she liked, so she set it aside to cool some more. "I have news too," Chrissy said, sounding happy to change the subject.

"Oh yeah?" Elnora asked, pulling the tea caddy closer so she could choose her next bag.

"Yep! Misty's replacement is in town, and we should be meeting him any day now."

"He?" Elnora asked.

Chrissy smiled. "Yes, 'he'. Apparently he's around our age and not too bad to look at," Chrissy smiled more deeply.

"When did he get here? Where's he from?" Elnora asked, selecting a ginger peach tea and placing it beside her cup.

"Friday night and McMinnville," Chrissy responded.

Elnora raised her eyebrows. "McMinnville? That's a bit further than expected."

Chrissy nodded in agreement. "Well supposedly he's not just Misty's substitute, he's looking at moving here permanently," Chrissy said, stirring her tea absently. "Hey--do you suppose Misty is …"

"Becoming a permanent housewife and stay-at-home-mom?" Elnora finished. "No way. She isn't the type, and she hates being bored. I'm sure she will be itching to get back to work long before her maternity leave is over."

"Yeah, I guess," Chrissy shrugged.

"What's his name?" Elnora took a long sip. Chrissy

shrugged again. "You don't know?" Elnora raised her eyebrows. "You know when he arrived, where he's from, and the exact proportions of his face, but you don't know his name?" Elnora teased her friend.

"Didn't catch that part," Chrissy blushed. They laughed together.

"Wow--fresh blood! That's kinda exciting," Elnora said, draining the last of her tea and opening the new packet.

"I'm pretty sure he will be all the town talks about for awhile here," Chrissy took a sip of her tea, then a deeper gulp.

"I'm pretty sure you're right," Elnora acknowledged, putting her new tea bag in her cup and filling it with water. "To a new adventure in our little town," she raised her mug, and Chrissy clinked it with her own.

Elnora spent the next hour with her friend, talking about whatever struck their fancy. By the time she got up to leave, she had drunk four cups of tea and Chrissy was still working on her second cup. Elnora helped her friend clear the table and wash the dishes before she left. Then she gave her friend a quick hug and walked back down the street to her own place. She hoped to get a lot of housework and a little bit of reading done before the end of the day, but somehow these plans got a little switched, as they often did, and as the sun sank below the horizon Elnora realized that she had only succeeded in tidying her bedroom and finishing half of her book. She prepared a quick dinner and took a long bath before bed, promising herself that she would get the rest of the housework done during the coming week, and falling asleep knowing that she probably wouldn't.

CHAPTER 5

"So we've been learning and practicing a lot of spelling patterns, haven't we?" Elnora asked her class, and a sea of heads bobbed their acquiescence. "Well can you think of how this can help us to spell words we haven't practiced? Because you know, there are a LOT of words out there, and we can't practice them all. So how can learning and practicing spelling patterns help us with those ones?" Almost every arm in the room shot up into the air, and Elnora smiled. "Ethan?" The arms dropped down amidst a collective sigh of disappointment. Ethan, a blonde boy with a big smile, sat up a little straighter.

"So we can be very good spellers!" Ethan asserted helpfully.

"That's very true, Ethan, we want to practice so that we can become very good spellers. And how can learning spelling patterns help with that?" Elnora asked again, prompting a new wave of arms in the air. "Joan?" Once again, arms dropped down amidst another loud sigh of disappointment. The girl in the back row with long dark hair gave a knowing, confident smile.

"So we can spell words we haven't practiced because they sound like words we have practiced," Joan said.

"That's exactly right, Joan. If we cannot practice spelling all the words, then knowing patterns that sound the same and are spelled the same can help you with words we haven't practiced," Elnora acknowledged. She saw understanding dawn on a handful of faces, while the rest retained a look of subtle confusion. It was time for an example. "Okay, let's say you're writing a story about a thief," Elnora started. Suddenly, her class was abuzz.

"Oh! Like the one who stole the eggs from Mrs. Busterson?" one voice piped up.

"It wasn't eggs, it was just one egg," another voice corrected.

"Who would steal an egg from someone's house?" a third voice asked.

"It wasn't an egg from a chicken, it was a special egg," a fourth voice explained.

"It was worth a million dollars!" a fifth voice offered excitedly.

"Class, settle down, settle down. We're not talking about Mrs. Busterson. It's spelling time, so let's get back to spelling, okay?" There was a little more noise, but they respected her and they quieted for her. "Like I was saying, you might be writing a story about a thief--maybe one who takes books from the library without checking them out," Elnora smiled as some of her students seemed horrified by this idea. "But let's say that you don't want to call him a thief. You want to call him a crook, which is another word for thief. We've never practiced spelling that word, have we?" Elnora asked her class, and saw them shake their heads. "We have practiced spelling 'book' though, haven't we?" The heads were bobbing now. "'Crook' and 'book' sound like each other, don't they? So we can use 'book' to help us spell 'crook'. How do you spell 'book'?" Arms shot up again, and many were accompanied by wiggling bodies and grunts for attention. Elnora found a quiet, still student and smiled. "Richie?"

"B … o … o … k," Richie announced proudly.

"Very good, Richie," Elnora wrote the word on her whiteboard. "So how do you think we would spell 'crook'?" More arms, though this time there was a little less squirming and grunting. "Molly?"

"C … o … o … k!" Molly guessed, shrugging. There were several muffled no's, and arms shot back up into the air. Elnora ignored the arms and instead nodded encouragingly at Molly.

"That's very good, Molly, and very close. But remember, we want to spell all the sounds we hear, so let's listen to all the sounds in the word. 'Crook'. What's the first sound?"

"Cr," Molly repeated slowly. Elnora nodded.

"Good. How do we spell that sound?"

"C … r?" Molly tried.

"That's right. What's the next sound?"

"Ook," Molly said.

"Right. And how do we spell that sound?" Elnora asked.

"O … o … k?" Molly asked.

"Perfect," Elnora said, writing the word on the board. The arms around the room fell again. "Do you guys see how this can work?" Heads bobbed again. "Good. Now take out your spelling papers and your pencils, because we are going to do our spelling dictation." There was a considerable amount of noise as desktops were opened and papers and pencils were retrieved. "Please number your papers from one to eleven,"

Elnora said. "Quickly," she added, "I'm going to give you the first word in exactly thirty seconds," she glanced up at the clock, and then back at her classroom full of busy students and smiled.

Blue Whale Cove Elementary was a u-shaped, red brick building that took up half the block. The classrooms were all arranged along the two arms of the building, while the administrative offices and large faculty lounge were at the base of the "u." At the end of the north arm was the gymnasium, which doubled as the theater for school productions. The outdoor space in the center of the "u" was the paved recess yard, while beyond the building was the large P.E. lawn.

The building was fifty years old, but it looked like it was less than ten years old because, like the rest of the town, it was kept in immaculate condition. The hallways were re-painted regularly so that they remained a crisp and perfect white, and the floors were kept clean and polished. While each teacher was left to decorate their own classroom as they desired and saw fit, the basic bones of each classroom were meticulously cared for and kept up by the janitors and estates team. Elnora was not alone in feeling that the beauty of the school generated a feeling of pride in the students that then pushed them to be more mindful of how they were treating the building. You were unlikely to see students purposefully rubbing their hands along the walls, leaving oil and dirt behind, or scuffing the floor with their shoes, putting gum on the walls or any of the other things that often contributed to the deterioration of elementary school buildings.

"Misty!" Elnora called out to the woman walking down the hallway in front of her. Misty Gunders turned slowly, revealing a very large pregnant belly. Elnora caught up to her and smiled warmly. "How are you doing?"

"Honestly? I'm exhausted, my ankles are swollen, I have to pee every five minutes, I'm always hungry but I don't ever know what I want to eat anymore and I just can't seem to get comfortable," Misty forced a tired smile as they turned together toward the faculty lounge. "I swear, if this baby doesn't come this week, I don't know what I'll do."

"I understand," Elnora held open the door into the lounge for her friend and waited patiently as Misty waddled through. The teacher's lounge was fairly large--nearly the same size as Elnora's five hundred square foot classroom--but it rarely had more than five faculty members in it at a time. It was decorated tastefully with warm colors, mostly reds and deep tans, with a couple of dark grays thrown in. There was a full kitchenette along the southern side of the room, while the remainder of the room was arranged like any popular coffee shop and lounge--groups of five or six comfy chairs placed around small tables staggered throughout the room. Elnora and her closest friends had an unspoken claim on the most comfortable set of chairs placed almost exactly at the center of the room, simply because they were the only faculty members who came into and used the lounge for nearly every break.

"I feel like a whale," Misty said, heading toward a place to sit.

"Well you don't look like one," Elnora said. "And I know you won't believe me, but I guarantee you that you don't look the way you feel. You look very cute," Elnora almost grimaced at the hard stare Misty gave her, and added, "And very pregnant. Here, sit here," Elnora indicated the large, comfortable red armchair just in front of them.

"You don't have to tell me twice," Misty sank gratefully

into the soft chair. The door opened and Chrissy stepped into the room, along with two more of their colleagues. Chrissy looked harried and exhausted.

"You okay?" Misty asked. Elnora held a fresh blueberry muffin and a glass of water out to Misty and looked up at her friend.

Chrissy nodded. "Becky brought a lizard in for show-and-tell. In her pocket," Misty and Elnora groaned in unison. "So basically show-and-tell became catch-the-lizard."

"Was it a pet lizard?" Elnora asked, suspecting she already knew the answer.

"Not *really*," Chrissy said cryptically. "It was a wild lizard she caught a week ago and has been keeping in her room."

"Do her parents know?" Misty asked, taking a small bite of her blueberry muffin.

"I don't know," Chrissy admitted, "But I don't think so."

"Wow, she's kept it alive for a week?" Elnora was impressed.

"Well enough for it to go racing around the classroom," Chrissy groaned.

"Well at least it was exciting," Misty sipped her water. "My students kept chattering about the burglary at Suzy's house."

"Uh-huh, mine too," Stan Drake spoke up. Stan taught fourth grade and often suggested that his students knew more about everyday affairs than he did. "It's actually pretty surprising how many details they've picked up."

"I've always said that you can get a perfect window into the adult conversations occurring in any home, simply by teaching the children who live in that home," Misty said. "I always know a household's political views right before an election," she shrugged and glanced over at Elnora.

"Well if I took my students' word at full value, Suzy

was robbed of chicken eggs that are worth a million bucks," everyone laughed along with her, though Chrissy's laugh sounded forced and uncomfortable. "It's just something new, and admittedly a bit odd," Elnora paused and everyone nodded. "Within a week or so, Suzy will have her check from the insurance company, she'll buy a new egg, something new and exciting will happen," she paused and winked knowingly at Misty, "And everyone will move on."

"My gosh, I hope I have this baby sooner than that," Misty looked wistfully down at her belly and rubbed it gently.

"Speaking of your maternity leave, I heard your replacement's in town," Chrissy sounded excited. "Any chance we'll get to meet him soon?" Misty shrugged.

"I haven't even met him yet. I heard he arrived Friday night and he's holed up at the Inn. I also heard," Misty smiled knowingly at Elnora and Chrissy, "That he's pretty decent to look at. Wink, wink, nudge, nudge," Misty kept smiling and Elnora laughed.

"Hey, don't look at me," Elnora said, motioning for Misty to back off. Misty giggled lightly.

"What, you're not into the tall, dark and handsome type?"

"I'm not into the 'dating in a fishbowl' type," Elnora said, and the three girls laughed. Stan rolled his eyes, sighed and backed away, stepping over to the coffee machine.

"I understand that," Misty said, rubbing her belly again. "That's why I went to Portland to fetch a husband," the girls laughed again.

"You are very wise," Elnora acknowledged, winking at Chrissy. "And you'll be an incredible mother--very, very soon." Misty smiled.

"Thanks, Elnora," Misty shifted in her chair.

Stan returned to the group, carrying a steaming mug of

coffee, and they chatted about various school-related things for awhile. Misty nibbled at her muffin and drank her water, continuing to rub her belly every few minutes. Elnora felt drawn to, and almost jealous of, the gesture--it looked so special for mother and child to have such a unique way to communicate with one another for nine months. She was mildly surprised by the emotion--it seemed sudden (she had been watching Misty for the past nine months) and though she was certain she wanted children, she also didn't feel a pressing, "my biological clock is ticking" urgency.

As the conversation dwindled into silence Misty sighed, glancing up at the clock. "Oh gosh--help me up. Recess is almost over, and it'll take me at least ten minutes to waddle back to my room." Chrissy and Elnora put their hands under Misty's elbows and helped her to lean forward and stand up. "See you guys at lunch?"

"We'll be there," Elnora confirmed, and Chrissy nodded. Misty pushed open the door and waddled out into the hallway.

"Gosh, I hope she has that baby soon," Chrissy muttered.

"Me too," Elnora agreed.

CHAPTER 6

Ten minutes after the dismissal bell had rung on Monday afternoon, Elnora unlocked the front door of her house and stepped inside. Within moments she had changed into her sweatpants, sweatshirt and hiking shoes and was back outside, locking her front door before moving toward Cedar Street and the beach and ocean beyond it.

As she walked, Elnora reviewed the last four hours of the school day, which had been nothing short of crazy. Not ten minutes after waddling back to her classroom after first recess in the morning, Misty had gone into labor. Or at least, so she had thought. The result of this sudden realization was a bit chaotic--she stopped in the middle of her lesson, sat down in the chair by her desk, and sent one of her students to fetch the assistant principal while she grabbed her phone and texted first her husband and then her midwife. By the time the assistant principal had arrived in her classroom, Misty's husband had left work on his way to get her, and

Misty's midwife responded that Misty needed to come by the birthing center as soon as possible, Misty's contractions had stopped. Everyone unanimously agreed that Misty should go ahead and start her maternity leave. Everyone except Misty, who had suddenly realized that she was about to have a baby and what exactly that meant--both physically and mentally. Going home and waiting meant that she would have plenty of time to worry about what was coming. Staying at school meant she could stay busy and perhaps forget what had just happened--and more importantly, what lay in her very near future.

The assistant principal and Misty's husband were both tough and tenacious, but Misty was even more so. After arguing for nearly a half hour in the hallway outside Misty's classroom, during which time Misty's students half-chatted with each other and half-listened to the adult conversation, Misty, her husband and the assistant principal reached a compromise. Misty could stay for today, if she promised to leave as soon as her contractions started up again--Braxton Hicks or otherwise--and if she promised that her maternity leave would start the following day regardless of what happened that day. Misty begrudgingly agreed, and so she returned to her class.

About halfway through her after-lunch period, Misty's students noticed something weird about their teacher. They noticed that Misty was breathing a little funny, talking a little funny and moving a little funny. By the time her forehead became beaded with sweat, Misty's students were fairly certain that something was very wrong with their teacher. Finally, one of the girls said, "She's in labor!" and one of the boys ran to get the assistant principal again.

The girls managed to convince Misty to stop teaching and sit down, but as soon as she did, her contractions stopped.

The assistant principal walked in just then, and found Misty looking quite normal, if not a little sweaty and winded. Once again, he tried to convince Misty to go on leave, but since she wouldn't admit that she had been having contractions, he was unable to garner her cooperation. He stormed off, back to the office and surely to call Misty's husband. Misty resumed her lesson and there were no further interruptions. Until the last recess.

During the last recess, Elnora pushed open the door into the faculty lounge and immediately knew that something was wrong. Misty was seated in the comfortable red armchair, but she was clearly anything but comfortable. She was chewing at her bottom lip, and despite her best efforts to stay still, she was fidgeting as much as any of Elnora's students did when it was two minutes until the dismissal bell. Elnora immediately rushed to her side, just as Stan brought Misty a cup of water.

"Misty?" Elnora asked. Misty turned her face toward her friend and managed a weak smile, her forehead beaded with sweat. "You're having contractions?" Elnora asked. Misty started to shake her head, then she looked again at her friend's kind eyes and nodded, slowly at first, then more firmly and urgently. "Stan, can you grab some sort of cloth and run it under some cold water?" Stan nodded and moved away. Just as he returned with a cold, wet rectangle of paper towel, Chrissy opened the door to the lounge. "Chrissy--here," Elnora held out Misty's phone and placed the paper towel on Misty's forehead. "Call Justin, tell him Misty's having contractions. Have you been timing them at all?" Elnora looked back at Misty, who shook her head. "No timing, but from the looks of it, things are pretty intense." Misty nodded again, fiercely this time. Chrissy nodded, took the phone and moved toward the window, only to return to Misty's side a moment later, gently picking up and placing Misty's right thumb over the home button to unlock the phone. Misty smiled weakly and then returned her right hand to her belly. A second later she sucked in her breath sharply and leaned forward, a subtle moan escaping her lips. Elnora placed a steadying hand on her shoulder. "Breathe, Misty. Deeply," Elnora glanced up at the clock and watched the seconds tick past. Finally, Misty relaxed and sank back into the chair. "That was forty-five seconds, Misty. I think it's safe to assume you're in labor." Misty turned wide, panicked eyes to her friend, and Elnora smiled gently in response. "You can do it, Miss. And just think, soon you'll have your precious baby girl in your arms," Misty's face relaxed into a smile, and she closed her eyes.

Justin Gunders arrived ten minutes later and together they all bundled Misty into his car, smiling and waving as they drove off. The rest of the school day--all forty-five minutes of it--was a complete loss, but at least the kids had something to talk about besides the burglary at Suzy Busterson's house. The moment the dismissal bell rang, a fifth grader stepped into Elnora's classroom and handed her a folded note. She opened it and read the clipped message. "Arrived at birthing center. Contractions stopped. Midwife says any moment now, just apparently not this one. Hugs, MG." Elnora shook her head and refolded the note. She had been totally certain that Misty was fully in labor--the contractions were close together, long and intense. But the same miracle that brought life into this world was also one of the biggest mysteries of this world, and one could never be completely sure.

Elnora crossed Main Street and a minute later her feet hit the soft, wet sand of the beach. She turned north and began to walk, closing the distance to the water on an angle until she was only five feet from the furthest reach of the rolling tide.

Despite the fact that this beach was usually always completely clean--no shells, no rocks, not even a scrap of seaweed, Elnora couldn't help but to look down as she walked. She sometimes drove an hour south and walked on the beach near Taft, hunting for agates as she walked. She didn't really have a purpose for doing this--although they did look pretty in the glass vases around her house--but something about hunting for treasures washed up on the beach was exciting and also somewhat addicting. Nonetheless, it had always proven pointless here in Blue Whale Cove, and Elnora forced her head back up just as she passed Suzy Busterson's house.

Elnora took in the expansive, single-story stone structure and considered the burglary again. Like everyone else she had spoken with, Elnora couldn't figure out why someone would want to go through the trouble--and the risk--of breaking into a house only to take one item that they couldn't easily sell. Not to mention the fact that they had supposedly walked right by some easy cash. Twice. It was easier to assume that Suzy had simply moved the pendant and then forgotten that she had. Except for the broken vase on her floor. If Suzy had just walked down that hallway an hour earlier and the broken vase wasn't there, it was safe to say that someone else had definitely been in her home. After all, china cabinet doors didn't just open by themselves, and vases didn't just spontaneously launch themselves from shelves and out into the air. Elnora giggled at the thought, then took a deep breath, sighed, and cleared her mind. She breathed in the salty sea air and felt the cool mist on her face. Aside from the excitement with Misty, she had experienced a fairly uneventful day in the classroom and had no students to ponder over. She decided instead to focus on the beautiful, rolling hills in the distance, and think of whatever drifted into her mind.

Elnora walked back in her front door an hour later. She kicked off her shoes on the small linoleum square that served as her entryway, poured herself a glass of cool water in the kitchen, and returned to her living room, dropping lightly back onto her couch. From her small coffee table she picked up her current book, the newest Jack Reacher thriller, and started reading from where she had left off as the sun slowly faded in the sky behind her.

CHAPTER 7

"Oliver, remember, you need to hold the point of the scissors down when you walk with them. Isabella? Please don't grab it out of his hand. Yes, I know he took it from you, but we're going to handle it with words," Elnora tried to convince the defiant young girl whose face was red with indignation. She could tell that she would probably have to step in and resolve the situation herself, but out of the corner of her eye she caught a bigger problem. "Dustin, remember, you have to stay seated in the painting corner until you are completely done. I can help you get a fresh cup of water, just please, stay seated," Elnora paused for a moment and took in the feeling of chaos that surrounded her.

As a 2nd grade teacher, Elnora was used to the feeling of controlled chaos. In fact, she was entirely fine with the fact that twenty energetic 2nd graders were a handful--it was a huge part of why she loved being a teacher. However, there was a distinct difference between controlled chaos and unruly chaos, and while the former never bothered her, the latter often meant that she was more of a wrangler than a teacher. What she was watching in her classroom right now was unruly chaos, and it was a particularly troubling case of it.

Somehow, Elnora got her students through the first period and out to the yard for recess. As soon as they were gone, Elnora made her way down the hall to the lounge for a relaxing cup of tea.

"Oh my gosh," Elnora sighed out loud as she stepped into the lounge.

Stan looked up from the soft armchair and grinned. "You too?" Stan asked. Elnora wrinkled her forehead at him. "We've just been talking about how today is more of a Monday than yesterday was; the kids are all a bit kooky," Stan explained. Elnora nodded.

"It must be a full moon," Chrissy offered from the chair beside Stan.

Elnora nodded again. "They're definitely energetic today," Elnora admitted. She poured hot water into a mug and grabbed a bag of chamomile tea, tearing it open and dipping the bag into her mug. She took her tea over to a chair by Stan and Chrissy and sank down gratefully. A moment later, the door slammed open and Theresa, a fourth grade teacher, rushed into the room, breathless.

"Did you hear?" Theresa puffed out, staring eagerly at the three of them. They all shrugged.

"Hear what?" Elnora asked. Theresa's eyes lit up.

"Misty had her baby girl this morning!" The words exploded out of her and for a moment, the room was filled with the sounds of delight and excitement.

"What's her name? How big is she?" Elnora managed to ask.

"Sophia Rose Gunders was born at 8:43 am, weighing in at 7 pounds, 3 ounces and measuring twenty inches exactly," Theresa shared.

"How adorable," Elnora acknowledged, and Chrissy nodded. Then Chrissy frowned.

"I totally forgot, what with how crazy the morning was, but with Misty gone on maternity leave, that means her replacement must be here. Has anyone seen him?" Chrissy asked, looking around. The others followed her lead, looking expectantly at everyone else. "No one has seen him?" They all shook their heads. Elnora watched disappointment cross her friend's face.

"Why don't you just stop by his classroom and say hi?" Theresa suggested, and Elnora saw the look of disappointment on Chrissy's face shift to fear.

"He's probably busy," Chrissy said unconvincingly. Theresa looked over at Elnora and smiled. Elnora returned the smile, but shook her head subtly, indicating she wasn't going to join in and tease her friend.

"That's true," Theresa acknowledged. "I guess Misty didn't prepare things as thoroughly as she had hoped to, so he actually has a lot to sort through and sort out. They had hoped she would be here all this week, turning the reins over to him, but obviously that didn't work out."

Elnora frowned. "That's a good point--why did he come in so late? Usually when they're planning out substitutes for long-term replacements like this, they have them come in much earlier. It's actually kind of weird that he only arrived … Friday? Was he even in the classroom with her yesterday?" Elnora looked around, catching shrugs and head shakes.

"I didn't even think about that," Theresa said. "But you're right, that *is* strange. It feels so last-minute, like Misty went out sick instead of on a planned maternity leave." Heads nodded in agreement, and then they all sat quietly for a few minutes, thinking.

"Oh no," Steve groaned, shifting in his chair. "They're coming back," he said darkly, and then smiled at the girls around him. "Here we go again ..." he stood and put his nearly-empty coffee mug into the sink. Chrissy and Elnora followed his lead, and they all stepped out into the hallway together, simultaneously taking deep breaths as they headed to their classrooms and the next period.

When her students had thundered out of the classroom for the final recess and Elnora decided she had to take a moment to clean up the utter disaster they had left behind, she was startled when Chrissy suddenly pushed open her door.

"He's like a ghost!" Chrissy's voice was half-awe and half-complaint.

"Who is?" Elnora asked, just as she removed a piece of paper from the floor and revealed a very large, very sticky and very shiny pile of glue and glitter. She sighed, though she couldn't help but smile as well. She stood and walked over to the cleaning cabinet, retrieving a roll of paper towels and some cleaning spray.

"Misty's replacement!" Chrissy said. Elnora muttered an "Oh" as she set to work on the floor. "He must be teaching during class time, of course, but as soon as class is dismissed he disappears! He's not in his classroom, he's not going to the faculty lounge, and no one in the office has seen him since he checked in."

"I'm sorry," Elnora said as she pulled the last of the glue

off the floor and walked over to deposit the whole soggy mess into the garbage. She looked up at her friend. "I know you were looking forward to meeting him. But he's going to be here for a while at the very least, and indefinitely at the very best," Elnora returned to collecting papers, pencils, crayons and other assorted items off the tables and floor, "So there's really no reason to go chasing him down on his first day." Chrissy looked mildly hurt, but Elnora knew that she hadn't truly upset her friend.

"I know, I know. It's just exciting--someone new! And so strange that we haven't seen him at all yet. We don't get a lot of excitement in this town," even as the words left her lips, Chrissy knew Elnora would tease her about it. Elnora didn't disappoint her friend.

"Let's see--in the space of three days we have had a home burglary, a new baby born and a substitute teacher come in from out of town. Not enough excitement, you say?" Elnora smiled at her friend, noticed two pencils that had been sharpened at both ends, and tossed them in the garbage. She then carefully placed the other items in their respective spots.

"I knew you were going to say that," Chrissy acknowledged, straightening the items on Elnora's desk. "I'm going to grab a quick soda before the next period--you coming to the lounge?" Chrissy asked, stepping over to the door. Elnora held her hands out, palms up, indicating toward her room.

"Not this time, sorry. I have to get this place straightened out before the next period," Elnora said, starting to push tables and chairs back into their proper positions. Chrissy nodded.

"Okay, see you later," Chrissy said, pushing through the door and back into the hallway. Elnora smiled at her friend's back and returned to organizing her classroom, noticing a small piece of tape that had somehow gotten attached to the wall, seven feet above the floor. She pulled a chair over to the spot, stepped up onto it, and pulled the tape down, looking around the walls and ceiling to verify that it was a solitary wanderer. She shook her head, marveling at the fact that something as impossible as this could've even occurred, especially without her noticing.

Elnora continued to work through her classroom, restoring order wherever possible. Experience told her that while order in their surroundings could not effectively eliminate all energetic tendencies in her students, it could help to calm them enough that they could get some class work done. Finally, after scouring her classroom several times and locating a few more markers without tops, several erasers that had been blackened with pencil markings and one more sticky pile of glittery glue, she returned to her desk. She had three minutes to spare until the next period bell, and as she surveyed her classroom she was happy to see that it actually looked normal to her.

Just as she turned to adjust her wall chart for her next lesson, Elnora saw a tall, dark shadow pass her window. She hurried over to the door, pushing it open and looking out down the hall. She just caught the back of him--he was tall and slender and he had short, dark brown hair--before the hallway was flooded with students and he was enveloped in the crowd.

As Elnora stepped back into her classroom, holding the door open for the flood of students coming in from the hallway, she smiled. She would have to tell Chrissy she had experienced a substitute teacher sighting.

CHAPTER 8

There were occasional days when Elnora chose not to go for her evening walk, especially when the weather was poor, but there were also the days when she knew she had to get out. That day was just such a day. The zoo that had been her class had left her feeling like an ineffective teacher, something she knew was entirely untrue. However, if she stayed at school or at home and thought about it, she would inevitably begin to question her teaching methods and success rates. For some reason, when she thought about tough days in the classroom while she was walking, she could spot and pick apart little clues that were helpful in reminding herself that it hadn't been her that had set the tone for the day, it had been her students. As an example, she recalled that the normally quiet and calm Ethan had been very erratic and energetic this morning. Elnora was willing to bet that Ethan's mom had left town for business the day before, as she often did, and Ethan's dad had been running a little behind this morning--allowing Ethan and his siblings to eat sugary cereal for breakfast (normally only allowed on the weekend) instead of the eggs, sausage, bacon, oatmeal or bagels, cream cheese and lox that normally made up their weekday breakfasts. Sasha had been a little more curt and rude to her friends than was normal, which likely meant that she hadn't gotten enough sleep the night before. Joan had been weepy, which often meant that she had encountered something in her studies that she didn't understand, but she was too proud to admit it and get the help she needed to sort it out. As Elnora ran through other clues and continued her deep breathing, she relaxed with the confirmation that it had just been "one of those days." It *was* interesting that unusual things tended to occur with a few of her students on the same day. It was also interesting that when unusual things occurred with a few of her students, unusual things also seemed to occur with other students in other classrooms on that same day. This sort of coincidence was something that Elnora had just learned to accept rather than question.

Elnora arrived at Main Street, but instead of crossing the street to the beach and continuing north along the water, she decided to turn north and continue her walk up through town. She absolutely loved walking along the beach, there was no denying that, but it was also refreshing to change things up every once in a while. She was always disappointed when she discovered that there was only one way to get to and from a place--it was nice to have multiple options, even if some took a little longer than others. Portland, for instance, could be a one and a half hour drive, a three hour drive or a nearly four hour drive, depending on which way she went. It's true that she rarely strayed from the route that took her one and a half hours, unless she was planning to go and stay overnight a couple days, but it was still nice to have options.

As Elnora approached Blue Whale Cove Treasures she slowed her pace until she was nearly standing still. She had always enjoyed window shopping in this town, especially in front of Treasures, with its colorful displays of blown glass. The current focus seemed to be jellyfish--they were everywhere in the store windows. There were tiny jellyfish dangling on delicate fish wire and larger jellyfish hanging from sturdier metal stands. Some of them were three inches long, leaving Elnora to marvel over the delicate handiwork that had gone into creating them and their nearly hair-thin tentacles, while some of them were more than a foot long, with tentacles thicker than crayons. A few were completely clear, but most of them were a riot of color, drawing the eye and stirring the automatic "I want one … or maybe five" that seemed to occur whenever one saw pretty things. Elnora caught the movement in the back of the shop and waved at Betty, the owner, before moving on.

Elnora kept a slightly faster pace as she moved in front of the windows of Blue Whale Cove Secrets. It was not because the jewelry there was any less stunning to look at, it was because Elnora trusted herself less to simply look and not buy at this store. It all lay in how useful she considered her purchases. Elnora had grown up with a mother who truly disliked "dust collectors"--pretty things that had no purpose other than to sit there and look pretty, and of course collect dust. Treasures was a store that mostly contained dust collectors--though Elnora would never tell Betty, or anyone else, that she thought this. There were a few bowls and glasses in stock, but they were so delicate that it was unlikely that they would be used often enough in Elnora's house to be worth purchasing. Secrets, however, was stocked with jewelry, and jewelry was very useful in Elnora's opinion. It could be worn to make one feel better and to make others smile. Elnora realized she may have glamorized the truth about jewelry and just how "useful" it really was, but nonetheless, she found it better not to linger in front of Secrets.

Elnora smelled the coffee well before she passed the shop, and it lingered in the air far past the bookstore and almost halfway past the inn restaurant. She smiled. She absolutely loved the smell of coffee, but she couldn't stand the taste. The smell, though--she would seriously consider buying a cup once in awhile just to enjoy the smell. Blue Whale Cove Coffee obtained fresh green beans from Colombia and roasted them on-site, which meant that they had some of the freshest, most richly flavored coffee around. It was no wonder that they had regular customers coming all the way down from Seattle--the country's coffee capital. These individuals were the true coffee connoisseurs, people who refused to settle for a good cup of coffee when there was great coffee to be had, even if it meant taking a bit of a drive.

Elnora finally passed out of the fragrant coffee cloud and continued on her walk north, past the inn. The inn was clearly doing a good amount of business--more than half the rooms were in use by the looks of the parking lot. One car, tucked in a back corner, caught her attention, and Elnora turned into the driveway to investigate closer. As she came nearer, Elnora was positive that she had seen it before, and not too long ago. It was an old car, a Toyota station wagon from the 1980s, and its coat of paint had long since faded to a matte gray. Apparently the hiker she had seen back at Cape Lookout last Sunday was staying in town. Elnora glanced around, half-expecting to see the hiker, while also quite certain that she most likely wouldn't. She walked back out of the driveway and onto the sidewalk, continuing past the inn office, the market and finally the cafe.

The sidewalk ended at the end of the cafe's property

line, and Elnora turned to clear the traffic in both directions before darting across the road. She climbed over a small dune and down the rocky hill to the beach, turning north to complete her walk.

An hour later, Elnora unlocked her front door, stepped into her house, kicked off her sandy hiking shoes in the small entryway, and closed and locked the door behind her. She felt relaxed, refreshed and hungry. She walked into the kitchen, flipping on the lights and grabbing a glass from the cabinet. She grabbed the water pitcher out of the refrigerator and poured herself a glass, drinking deeply and then sighing. She took salad greens, carrots and cucumbers from the fridge and fixed herself a quick salad, topped with balsamic vinegar and olive oil.

Elnora ate her dinner in the living room while watching a romantic comedy movie. Two hours later, she was in bed, smiling as she thought of Misty and her newborn baby girl, spending their very first night home together.

CHAPTER 9

When the dismissal bell rang on Wednesday afternoon, Elnora lingered in her classroom long after it was empty. It was a rare occasion: she would not be going on her walk this afternoon. Instead, she would be doing something much, much better, and she found it difficult to contain her excitement as she glanced up at the clock every few minutes. She was going to visit Misty and her new baby girl at their home.

Misty had first reached out the evening before to ask Elnora when she was going to visit, and Elnora had insisted that she wanted Misty, her husband and her baby to have several days alone together, to bond as a new family. Misty chuckled into the phone and reminded Elnora that in their small town, there truly was no such thing as alone time. Misty had already introduced Sophia to over thirty Blue Whale Cove residents--mostly women who insisted that they were just bringing over meals (which they did) and assured

Misty that they were available to help with the house cleaning if needed, so that Misty could spend all her time bonding with her new daughter and wouldn't have to worry about a thing. Of course, no one would mind if Misty asked them to hold the baby while she used the restroom.

Though Elnora had meant to be polite by waiting a week before visiting, she realized that if she didn't get over to Misty's soon, not only would she be the absolute last person in Blue Whale Cove to meet little Sophia Rose, but she may very well upset her friend by denying her company and praise. So Elnora had promised Misty that she would come by after class today--right around 4:00 pm. Misty said this was perfect, because it would give her time to take a nice nap after lunch and still have time to prepare for Elnora's arrival. Elnora had plenty to do in her classroom until then, so she set to work with her lesson planner.

Elnora was fairly engrossed in planning out a geography lesson when her door opened and someone entered. She started when her visitor cleared his throat, and she jumped up to face him. He was tall and slender--about six foot two and one hundred eighty pounds, with soft, dark brown hair and a very handsome face. He moved forward slightly, his hands held out in front of him in an apologetic gesture.

"I'm sorry, I didn't mean to startle you," he explained. Elnora shrugged and shook her head.

"It's okay, I was a little more involved in my thoughts than usual," Elnora smiled gently, and he smiled in return. Now that he was standing before her, Elnora silently agreed with the reports she had heard. He was very handsome. His hair was close-cropped and neat, and his face was defined by the strong jawline that most women found incredibly attractive. His eyes were a warm brown color--and they were focused on hers. Elnora cleared her throat and looked away, down at the floor.

"My name is Kevin, Kevin Hiller," he stuck out his hand and Elnora placed her own in it, allowing him to gently press and shake it. His hand felt warm and soft, and she let it go reluctantly. He paused, for just a fraction of a second, looking carefully into her face. "Have I seen you … around?" he asked. Elnora nodded. "At Cape Lookout?" Elnora nodded again. "I was coming and you were going?" Elnora nodded one more time. "Well then, it's nice to officially meet you. I'm the substitute filling in for Misty. I heard that no one believed I really existed, so I'm making the rounds and introducing myself," Elnora heard the tremor in his voice and realized he was slightly nervous. She smiled again.

"It's nice to meet you, Kevin. I'm Elnora," she felt the heat rising to her face, and looked down at the papers on her desk. "So--how do you like Blue Whale Cove?" She tried hard to make her voice sound completely calm and natural, and wondered why it was such a struggle to do so. She started to sort the papers into piles.

"I've always liked Blue Whale Cove," Kevin said matter-of-factly. Elnora looked up, surprised.

"You've been here before?"

"Oh yeah, many times, though it's been more than fifteen years since I was last here. My aunt lived in Blue Whale Cove until she passed. We visited her every month or so over the last ten years of her life," Kevin explained quietly. Elnora's mind raced--trying to connect the dots. Could it be …

"Samantha Hiller?" Elnora asked. It was Kevin's turn to look surprised. "I've grown up my whole life here," Elnora explained, "And I'm sure you know that everyone here knows everyone else and everything that happens in town." Kevin nodded.

"That I do know. Aunt Sam loved to talk my ear off with all the town gossip--who was getting married, who was having a baby, who had moved into town, who had left town, who was sick and with what ailments, who had passed on, who visited who and how often (a bragging point, of course), how everyone decorated their house and landscaped their yards, and anything and everything else that came to mind," Kevin smiled at what was obviously a fond memory. "I've spent my whole life in a big city, where few people even know their next door neighbors, so it was kind of fun to hear stories from a town where everyone knew everyone else so well. Aunt Sam made it interesting, too, like she was telling old folk tales."

"She was a sweetheart," Elnora remembered the kindly old woman who loved to bake--apparently 24/7--and then share her delicious treats with everyone. The whole town had grieved when she had passed fifteen years ago, and even though Elnora had been only fifteen at the time she remembered it well. "I remember she made the best, juiciest and flakiest apple pie I've ever tasted," Elnora added wistfully. Kevin nodded.

"She won several baking competitions when she was younger. She even toyed with the idea of opening a bake shop in town for a brief time, but she just didn't have the capital so she didn't pursue it seriously."

"I didn't know that," Elnora was surprised. The residents of Blue Whale Cove prided themselves on helping one another, and doing so in such a way that it never came across as charity. "If she had told just about anyone in town, I'm sure she would've gotten the help she needed to open a bake shop," she said, voicing her thoughts. Kevin smiled.

"She knew that, and that's exactly why she didn't say

anything to anyone," Kevin said. "Too proud, you know," he explained.

"So true," Elnora acknowledged. She moved a couple more papers into their appropriate piles and glanced back up at him. "So, I heard that you were looking at staying on, not just as a substitute."

"I'm thinking about it. I always liked it out here--it's so much smaller, and so much quieter."

"It is that--especially if you're accustomed to the noise and crowd of big cities," Elnora said, and then she glanced up at the clock and saw the time. "Oh gosh, I'm so sorry," she quickly shifted the piles of paper on her desk into one of her drawers and brushed a hand over the desktop to clear it of eraser debris, "I have to run, Misty is waiting to introduce me to Sophia Rose," Elnora smiled. "It was nice to meet you, Kevin, and I look forward to seeing you around. So sorry--I really have to run!" Elnora grabbed her bag from the floor under her desk, pushed open her classroom door and trotted down the hallway and out to the parking lot to her car, leaving Kevin to look after her with a smile of amusement on his face.

Elnora pulled into Misty's driveway at exactly 4:00 pm, and she gently rapped on the door at exactly 4:01 pm. Misty opened the door, looking both exhausted and blissfully happy, and pulled Elnora into the house.

"You look great," Elnora whispered.

"Thank you," Misty replied with a tired smile.

"How are you doing?"

"I'm absolutely exhausted, but I'm very happy and I wouldn't have it any other way," Misty admitted, leading

Elnora through the foyer and into the living room. She indicated to the couch and Elnora took a seat. "Can I get you something to drink?" Misty stood before her friend and gestured toward the kitchen.

Elnora shook her head. "I'm fine. Please sit," Elnora patted the couch next to her and Misty gratefully sank onto the cushion. Elnora looked around the pristine living room, which consisted of a black leather couch and matching black leather armchair, a beautiful walnut coffee table, two matching walnut side tables, and a walnut entertainment cabinet, upon which sat a 70" television set. There were a couple small, decorative pieces, but the only indication that a baby was in the house was a small burp cloth thrown over the arm of the armchair. "Where's Sophia?" Elnora asked.

"Justin took her to change her diaper just before you arrived, they'll be back any second," Misty smiled.

"Wow, you've already got him changing diapers?"

"Oh Elnora, he's wonderful," Misty said proudly. "He even gets up to change her in the middle of the night. He says he wants me to get as much sleep as possible. I'm soaking it in while I can--next week he returns to work and I have a feeling his batteries will start running much lower." Elnora laughed. The next moment, Justin walked into the living room with a small, warm bundle held gently in his arms. He looked inquisitively at Elnora, who smiled and nodded back eagerly. Justin came to Elnora and placed the small, warm bundle in her outstretched arms.

Elnora pulled the bundle close and stared down at the beautiful baby girl sleeping in her arms. She marveled over the tiny little lips, the perfect little nose, the soft, delicate ears, and the teeny little fingers. Misty chuckled lightly.

"You're going to get a crick in your neck," Misty said.

"It's worth it," Elnora smiled, then looked up at her

friend. "She's absolutely beautiful, Misty. So perfect." Misty smiled, a glowing smile of motherly pride.

"It's really amazing, you know," Misty said quietly, "You want to become a mother for so long, and then when you find out you're pregnant you have nine *long* months to get prepared for actual motherhood. And I promise you, you really think you're prepared. You cannot wait to meet your baby, and you already know that you will love them more than anything in the whole world," Misty sighed happily. "And then this … *amazing* being is placed in your arms and you realize that you were not prepared at all, and that you love her even more than you had imagined you would. It's so overwhelming, and so perfectly wonderful. I mean--I'm a *mom*, Elnora," Misty sounded awed as she looked down at her daughter's face.

"Yes, you are," Elnora said, looking up into her friend's face and then back down at the baby in her arms.

"It's the hardest thing I've ever done," Misty confessed, "And there's definitely many more challenges to come, but it's also the most rewarding thing I've ever done."

"Do you need any help?" Elnora asked. "What can I do to help?"

Misty leaned forward, placing an arm on her friend's leg. "Nothing, Elnora. I don't need anything. I have so many people stopping by and dropping off food that I won't have to cook again for a year, and every time someone stops by they end up cleaning or organizing something for me. I haven't had to worry about anything except enjoying Sophia and sleeping as much as I can." Misty smiled.

"Well if anything comes up, please tell me. I'll make a run for diapers, come over just to hold her for you so you can rest--or take a shower--whatever you need," Elnora looked back down at the beautiful girl in her arms.

"Thanks, Elnora. Maybe you can just come by every once in awhile to hang out, I'd like that," Misty said.

Elnora nodded. "Of course I'll do that," Elnora smiled at her friend. They both stared down at Sophia for several minutes. "By the way, I just met your substitute," Elnora said quietly.

"Oh yeah?" Misty asked, the faintest hint of concern lacing her voice. "Does he seem nice? I mean, do the kids like him?"

"Even if they adore him, you know perfectly well that they will be overjoyed when you return," Elnora said firmly, looking at her friend. Misty shrugged.

"It doesn't really matter, I guess, since I won't return before the school year ends and I'll have a whole new class in the fall," Misty rearranged her daughter's blanket, exposing ten delicate and perfect little toes for just a second.

"That's true," Elnora agreed, "But then you've never had a shortage of ex-students coming back to visit you." Misty smiled widely in agreement. "You're a great teacher, Misty, and no substitute will change that." Misty placed a grateful hand on her friend's arm.

"So what's he like?"

"He's very nice," Elnora offered. Misty laughed.

"How very vague. What's his name? How old is he? What's he look like?" Elnora suspected Misty knew the answers to her questions--it was likely that she and Kevin had met at least once to go over her lesson plans--but she wanted to see Elnora's reaction to describing her new co-worker. Elnora sighed.

"Kevin is very tall and handsome," Elnora admitted. "I think Chrissy will be thrilled, when she finally meets him. They would make a cute couple, both a little timid but very kind," Elnora shrugged again. Misty frowned, this was clearly not the direction she had intended the conversation to go in. "Did you know that Samantha Hiller was his aunt?" Misty shook her head. "That's why he is putting in for a permanent transfer--he fell in love with the town during all his visits here and now he would like to stay." The baby shifted in Elnora's arms, grunting ever so slightly, and both women fell silent. As they watched, Sophia gently blinked her eyes open, looking up at the two women watching her. Elnora talked gently with the baby, watching the tiny, deep brown eyes take in everything. Eventually, Sophia became restless and Elnora handed her over to her mother, who nursed her for a long while. With a full belly, Sophia drifted back off to sleep, and Elnora gratefully accepted her back into her arms.

Elnora and Misty continued to chat, in hushed tones, for another hour. Finally, after what seemed to be a wink of time, Elnora sighed--a long, sad sound.

"You have to go?" Misty asked, her voice both sad and amused.

"I have to go," Elnora agreed. "I wish I didn't, but if I don't eat dinner soon …"

"You could eat here," Misty offered, only half-joking. "Goodness knows I have enough!"

Elnora smiled and shook her head. "I wouldn't dream of touching your stash," Elnora whispered, lifting Sophia closer so she could breathe in her wonderful, baby smell. "That's for you, so you can enjoy this as thoroughly as you deserve," Elnora took another deep breath and softly kissed Sophia on her forehead. Then she sighed again, deeply, and gently passed the soft, warm bundle back to Misty. Misty gazed down at her sleeping daughter and then up at her friend.

"I mean it, you can stop by as often as you want."

"I will, I promise," Elnora said, pushing off the couch and standing up, grabbing her bag from the floor beside her.

"You take care of yourself, so you can take care of her," Elnora leaned over and hugged Misty around the shoulders, careful of the baby between them. Misty nodded.

"I will."

"And promise you'll let me know if you need anything," Elnora added as she walked over to and opened the front door.

"I promise."

"She's really beautiful, Misty. You did very well," Elnora gave her friend one last smile, and then walked into the foyer and out the door, pulling it gently closed behind her.

CHAPTER 10

Elnora and her students breezed through their Thursday morning writing class and were all surprised when the bell announcing first recess rang through the building. "Already?" one student said, while another complained, "I want to finish my story!" Elnora smiled and told them that she loved hearing that from them, but it was also important to get outside and exercise. They agreed, although somewhat half-heartedly, put away their writing journals and pencils, and went outside for recess. Elnora headed to the teacher's lounge and prepared herself a cup of tea. She had just sat down in the comfy red armchair when the door opened and Chrissy came in, her face a mask of confusion.

"I don't know what to do," Chrissy announced, standing just inside the door and throwing her hands into the air.

"About what?" Elnora asked, taking another sip of tea. Chrissy walked to the sink, grabbed a clean mug and saucer, filled the mug with hot water, grabbed a tea packet, and came to sit across from her friend.

"Jeffrey is still writing backwards. Every single letter, every single word. I've tried everything I can think of--tracing paper, clay, sand raking, all of it. He's still writing backwards," Chrissy sighed, setting down her mug and tearing open her tea packet.

"That's pretty amazing. How is the formation? The size, the spacing, the shape?" Elnora asked. Chrissy shrugged.

"It's absolutely perfect. He would be my best handwriter if the letters and words weren't backwards," Chrissy dipped her tea bag into her mug, moving it up and down until the water turned amber brown.

"He *is* your best handwriter," Elnora corrected. Chrissy looked at her, crinkling her eyes and forehead in confusion. "How does he read and spell?" Chrissy shrugged again.

"He reads fine. He has the normal sort of difficulties decoding new words and memory words, but he reads fine. Spelling is the same--no real problem."

"You said it--there's no real problem," Elnora smiled. "If he's got perfect letter size, shape and spacing and he's reading and spelling just fine, I wouldn't worry about the writing backwards bit," Elnora took another sip of tea.

"But ..." Chrissy started, and then stopped. She couldn't think of what else to say.

"Leave it alone," Elnora pressed. "I'm willing to bet that if you leave the writing alone, except to acknowledge what's right about it--the size, shape and spacing--he will fix it himself. And probably soon," she paused and saw the light begin to show in Chrissy's eyes. "He seems like a smart kid," she said and Chrissy nodded in agreement, "And I'm sure that he will notice for himself that his letters and words are backwards and then he will want to fix it. I bet you it won't even be a major struggle for him. If he's pressed into fixing it, however, he may continue to write them backwards on purpose--just to prove that no one tells him what to do."

"That's brilliant," Chrissy said, bobbing her tea bag up and down in her mug a few more times, then removing it and placing it on the saucer. "I'm going to try it. At least I can stop worrying about it for a little, just to see."

"Good idea," Elnora said, taking another sip of tea.

"Hello," Chrissy's voice was soft and low, and Elnora looked up at her in surprise. But Chrissy's eyes were not on Elnora's face, they were above her and to her left. Elnora turned and saw Kevin standing in the doorway, his hand gently holding the door open.

"You can come in, you're allowed," Elnora offered and Kevin smiled.

"I was looking for Stan, but it seems he's not in here," Kevin explained.

"He popped in just long enough to grab a cup of coffee and then bolted out again," Elnora said. "Have you checked his classroom?"

Kevin nodded. "I did. It's okay--I'll catch him later," and he was gone. Elnora turned to Chrissy, who had a big grin on her face.

"He's pretty cute," Chrissy giggled. Elnora sighed.

"Have you spoken with him yet? I mean, aside from that 'hello' just now?" Elnora asked

"A little. He stopped by my classroom yesterday afternoon to introduce himself. I said 'hello' and told him my name," Chrissy shrugged and then tested her tea.

"That a girl," Elnora teased.

"I'm trying," Chrissy said earnestly. "But the truth is ... well, I know he's good-looking and all, but I'm not entirely sure he's my type."

Elnora raised her eyebrows. "You've said three words to him and already decided he's not your type?"

Chrissy nodded. "It's just a feeling. I mean, I could be wrong--every time I see him I kinda wish I'm wrong--but it just doesn't *feel* right," Chrissy waved her hands, as if to drive her point home. "I'm not describing this very well, am I?"

"Not really, no," Elnora smiled. "But I think I know what you mean anyway. Although I think you should try talking to him a little longer before you dismiss him," Elnora shrugged, "Especially since you are obviously very attracted to him."

Chrissy blushed. "That bad, huh?"

Elnora nodded, sipping more of her tea. "Pretty obvious, yeah. But I think he may be one of those guys who's flattered, rather than driven off."

Chrissy looked at her friend. "You do?"

Elnora nodded. "I do. But really, you should talk to him. What's the worst that could happen?"

Chrissy paled. "I could die of shame."

"Sure you could," Elnora replied sarcastically.

Chrissy laughed. "Okay, okay. I'll try."

Elnora drained the last of her tea. "You do that. Well, wish me luck--I'm trying a new geography seminar. I'm hoping that if I get the students up and moving around, creating a map instead of just looking at one, it'll be more interesting," Elnora rinsed her mug and put it in the dish drain to dry.

"Good luck!" Chrissy called after her, sipping a little more of her tea before setting the mug on the counter next to the microwave. There was a 50% chance she would finish her tea later, when it was completely cool and she could chug it in three gulps.

"See you at lunch," Elnora called over her shoulder as

she and Chrissy stepped into the hallway and started toward their classrooms, dodging a stream of energetic elementary schoolers. Chrissy wiggled her fingers over her shoulder in response, and then ducked in through her classroom door.

Elnora stepped away from the hard, packed wet sand and onto the softer, dry sand, taking a seat and pulling off her hiking shoes to empty them out. As she tipped the right shoe over, a small waterfall of sand fell to the ground, creating a tall pile that was instantly decimated by a gust of wind. Elnora brushed the sand off her right sock and then grabbed her left shoe as it started to roll away, tucking it under her left leg as she put her right shoe back onto her foot and tied it. Then she did the same with her left shoe, turning it over and creating a small sand waterfall and a miniature sand dune before brushing the sand off her sock and returning her shoe to her foot. A voice behind her, subtly muted by the wind, startled her.

"Collecting?" Elnora turned to see Kevin standing there, wearing dark gray sweatpants and a black, long-sleeved shirt with black Nike tennis shoes. His short hair was being pushed and pulled by the wind, which made him look all the more relaxed and comfortable. "I'm sorry; I tried to make more noise as I approached this time, so I wouldn't startle you, but the wind makes that sort of difficult."

"Kevin--hello," Elnora stood and faced him, brushing sand off her backside and legs.

"So, a fellow hiker and daily walker?" Kevin asked, and Elnora nodded.

"Every day, if I can make it."

"Me too. Helps to clear my head," Kevin looked out

toward the ocean and took a deep breath. After a moment, he looked back at Elnora. "Are you wrapping up or just getting started?"

"Just getting started. I'm used to getting sand in my shoes, but that was a little too much for comfort. It made everything lumpy."

"Can't have that," Kevin agreed. "I'm heading north--would you like to walk together?" Kevin asked, then scrambled to politely give her an out, "I mean, only if you want. I realize you may enjoy walking alone and I don't want to impose."

"No, no, some company would be nice," Elnora turned north and fell into stride beside him.

"So, you grew up in Blue Whale Cove," Kevin said, his voice being pushed forward by the wind so that Elnora captured a strained, muffled version.

"I did," Elnora nodded. "And you grew up where--Portland?"

"Beaverton, but close enough," Kevin waved his hand as if to dismiss the notion that there was much difference between the two.

"How did you end up in McMinnville?" Elnora asked, the wind swirling her hair into her face so it was hard to see Kevin beside her. She pushed her hair back from her face with one hand and pulled the hood of her rain jacket up with the other hand.

"I got my BS in education at Western Oregon, and I took a job in the McMinnville School district because I was ... seeing someone who grew up in McMinnville and wanted to live and work in that area. It didn't work out between us pretty much right after we made the move, but I stayed in the district for awhile because I was already set up and I figured it would be good teaching experience. I always planned to try and transfer out here, it just took a little longer than I had anticipated. You?"

"I graduated from OSU and came right back home to work," Elnora admitted. Kevin smiled and nodded.

"I understand why--it's a pretty special place," Kevin looked back toward the town. "I've never seen another place quite like it. It reminds me of the town in 'The Truman Show' … Sea-something."

"Seahaven?" Elnora offered.

"Yeah. It's so well-kept and everyone is so friendly."

"That's certainly why I love it," Elnora admitted. "Have you traveled much--I mean, besides coming here to visit your aunt?"

"A good bit around the state, not much more than that. I went to New York once, and down to California a couple times, that's about it. How about you?"

"A bit. I've also been to New York and California, as well as New England and the Southeast. There's no place quite like home, though," Elnora stepped around Kevin, moving further west toward harder-packed sand. "I have to tell you, it's kind of weird that you came to visit your aunt so often but we've never met before. I had never even heard of you before, no offense."

"None taken," Kevin motioned toward the waves and they both stepped farther east, out of the way of a particularly vigorous wave that was creeping ever closer. It finally reached its limit and rolled back to the sea, and they moved together back toward the harder, wet sand. "The truth is that Aunt Sam wasn't much of a gossip … about personal things," Kevin emphasized the last three words. "And we spent most of our visits just sitting in her house. I would read while she baked, and then we would sit together and play board games and chat for hours."

"That sounds very nice," Elnora agreed, stepping further east again to dodge another wave. Kevin matched her movements and stepped out of her way.

"It was nice. Occasionally, while she was napping, I would sneak out and come down here to walk, which is probably when I fell in love with the place." They walked on in silence for several more minutes, enjoying the sound of the whistling wind and the crashing waves. "You know, Aunt Sam taught me to read," Kevin said suddenly. Elnora looked over and caught the fond smile on his face. "I mean, I could "read", you know, sounding out the letters and the words and all, but I wasn't *really* reading. I did what I had to in order to get by, but stories and books held no pleasure for me and I struggled every day with the material I couldn't understand," Kevin shook his head. "At eight years old, I was surrounded by friends who loved to read for pleasure and I couldn't understand it. Aunt Sam found out, I can't remember how, and she started introducing me to the best stories she could think of. She read me *Magic Treehouse, Charlie and the Chocolate Factory, Warriors, Harry Potter, Ender's Game*--some of my favorite stories still to this very day. She helped me to understand and fall in love with the stories. And then I took off on my own--reading anything and everything I could get my hands on."

"What's your favorite now?" Elnora asked.

Kevin laughed. "I don't have a favorite, I have fifty--maybe even a hundred."

"I know what you mean, I'm the same way," Elnora admitted. "I love to read."

"Do you have any favorites?" Kevin asked and Elnora smiled.

"Just about a hundred of them. I've gone through phases--there was a long one when I was in my late teens and I loved anything and everything by Stephen King. Now I can't read it--it's just too creepy for me. I enjoy reading Michael Crichton, David Baldacci, Dan Brown, James Patterson, Janet Evanovich, John Grisham, Elmore Leonard, David Weber, Steve Berry, Lee Child, just to name a few."

"Wow, that's a pretty good spread there, seems like you prefer mystery and action?" Elnora shrugged and nodded. "I've read most of those authors myself. And of course there's Lee Child--you're a Reacher fan, eh?" Kevin asked.

"The biggest," Elnora gushed, nodding. "He's not like a superhero--all perfect and selfless and all that jazz. He's just … a guy who happens to lead a lifestyle that naturally brings him into contact with many individuals. Some of these individuals are less than honest, and he refuses to let it slide. I have to admit that I really love how he goes around acting like he doesn't care, not about anything or anyone, but then when he notices things that aren't the way they should be, he won't turn a blind eye to the situation and he always does something about it, often putting others' safety and well-being before his own. Plus, he's confident, intelligent and incredibly successful in his efforts to take out the 'bad guys.' He epitomizes the exact reason I love to read fiction--to see the good guys win, the bad guys lose and to experience some sense of vindication."

"I can understand that," Kevin said. "I like Reacher too. And Oliver Stone of the Camel Club."

"You know Oliver Stone?" Elnora looked surprised--almost like she believed that no one else could have possibly read the same bestsellers she read. Kevin laughed.

"Yeah--I read the Camel Club series long before I even heard of Lee Child or Jack Reacher. I got hooked on mystery and action novels for much the same reason you just explained--you hear about or even see bad things happening all the time in the world around you, but you rarely get to see the vindication. And maybe the vindication doesn't even always happen, but then that's the real world for you. It's nice to escape sometimes to other worlds--where the good guy usually wins and you get all the vindication your heart desires." Elnora nodded in agreement. "Now do your movie preferences follow along with this--with a leaning toward action and adventure?"

"Sort of," Elnora said, tucking stray hair back under her hood. "I like action and adventure films when there's also a streak of humor running through them, like you see in *Die Hard*, *Shooter*, the three newest *Mission Impossible* films, most *Avengers* or *Marvel* films, the newer *Star Trek* films, many of the *Fast and Furious* films and so on. But I also like romantic comedies, like *Leap Year* and *27 Dresses*, and of course, *The Princess Bride*."

"That *is* a good film. Actually, all of those are," Kevin corrected.

"You sound surprised."

"Not surprised, no," Kevin shrugged, "Just impressed at the breadth of your collection, and how many are in common with my own."

"Well then maybe I should mention that I also love some kid's films, like *Holes*, *Kung Fu Panda*, *How to Train Your Dragon*, and *Harry Potter*," Elnora said.

"I might argue that the *Harry Potter* series isn't really a 'kid's film' series, it's an 'anyone who likes a darn good fantasy story' film series," Kevin pointed out. "But aside from that, I don't think there's anything wrong with enjoying a few, well-made kid's films either." Elnora smiled. She was enjoying this conversation, despite the fact that she had to raise her voice a bit more than normal in order to project over the wind and she was accustomed to walking alone most of the time so she could spend time with her thoughts.

"You know," Kevin said thoughtfully, "I'm enjoying this," he smiled, and Elnora matched his smile. "I normally walk alone because it's nice to just enjoy the landscape and think," Elnora nodded in agreement, wondering if Kevin could read thoughts, "But this has been nice. I hope you don't mind, but I sorta look forward to running into you more on our walks."

"I don't mind, and I agree," Elnora said. They walked on, all the way to Elnora's usual turning point and then back south toward town, continuing to chat as they walked. When they reached the intersection of Cedar Street and Main Street, Kevin stopped and turned toward Elnora.

"I guess this is where we part ways," Kevin said and Elnora nodded.

"Yep. You're at the inn, right?" Elnora asked. Kevin smiled.

"No secrets in this town, huh?"

"Actually, I saw your car when I walked by the inn on Tuesday. It's kinda distinctive," Elnora tried to sound impressed, rather than sarcastic. Kevin smiled proudly.

"Bought that car in my junior year of high school, and it's been running ever since. It's a machine!" Kevin did sound genuinely impressed. "It's an ugly machine," he conceded, "But it's a machine. I'm hoping it'll last another couple years at least--time enough for me to finish saving up for my next 'new to me' purchase."

"That is pretty impressive," Elnora admitted. She had also purchased a used car in high school, but then as soon as she had finished college and obtained her teaching position she had traded it in for a new car. She appreciated all the "bells and whistles" that came with a newer car, but mostly she just loved the dependability.

"I'd like to tell you that it's all because of me and my excellent skills as a mechanic, but that wouldn't be true at all. It really is a good car," Kevin sighed wistfully and Elnora couldn't help but laugh. Kevin glanced at her and smiled. "Well thank you again, for the nice conversation and lovely walk. I really did enjoy it."

"I did too. See you at school tomorrow," Elnora said, turning and walking off up Cedar Street. Kevin watched her for a moment and then turned and headed north up Main Street, back to the inn. Elnora didn't really know what had just happened, but she did know that she wouldn't mind if it happened again.

CHAPTER 11

"Billy, don't forget your coat," Elnora called after a young boy who was trying to sneak out the classroom door in his t-shirt. "It's chilly today!" Elnora glanced out the windows at the thick fog enveloping the school, and the town. The boy sighed loudly, stepped two feet to the right, grabbed his coat from the peg it was hanging on, and continued out the door into the hallway. Elnora walked up and down the aisles, pushing in chairs and straightening desks.

"You coming?" Chrissy asked through the open doorway. Elnora nodded.

"Be right there," Elnora confirmed, pushing in another chair. Chrissy smiled and disappeared. A few moments later, Elnora heard the door to the faculty lounge swing open and then closed. It was a testament to just how quiet the building became when the students all exited it--the faculty lounge was at least a hundred feet, and one hallway curve, away.

Elnora pushed the last few chairs in, grabbed three pencils and one marker off the floor and returned them to their containers on the writing shelf, and made her way out of the classroom, down the hallway and into the faculty lounge.

As she pushed open the door, Elnora suddenly stopped short. The lounge was far more full than normal, with apparently every single available faculty member packed inside. Kevin was standing in the middle of the crowd, looking mildly uncomfortable.

"Oh good, you're here!" Lexi, from the front office, stepped over to Elnora, gently pulling her into the room and closing the door behind her. "We just wanted to take a moment to formally welcome Kevin to the team," Lexi motioned at Kevin, who smiled nervously at the crowd, "And to congratulate him on surviving his first week--not as a substitute teacher, but as a provisional teacher here at Blue Whale Cove Elementary." There were pleased "ohs" around the room, and many heads nodded in acknowledgement. Lexi turned to Kevin and addressed him directly, "We're glad you're here, Kevin, and we look forward to continuing to see you around, hopefully for a long while." Kevin nodded and managed a quiet "Thank you."

The main event now over, the crowd of teachers immediately began to disperse--some returning to their classrooms, some grabbing coffee, tea or snacks, and others moving into smaller groups around the room to chat. Kevin received a few personal welcomes, looking far more comfortable with a small line of individuals than he had with a large group. Elnora stood a few feet away, watching. Finally, the line disappeared and Kevin stood alone, looking slightly shell-shocked.

"You love surprises, don't you?" Elnora asked. Kevin nodded.

"Especially when there are large crowds involved," Kevin rubbed his hand over his forehead and face. "At least that's over," Kevin said, then leaned in a little closer and lowered his voice, "Though I'm pretty sure I don't remember the names of any of the people I just met," he stood up straight and widened his eyes momentarily, in faux horror. Elnora laughed.

"I don't think anyone would. Don't worry, we'll help you," Elnora made a serious face. "So … what's my name?" she asked, and they both smiled. Chrissy stepped over to join them. "This is Chrissy," Elnora said, indicating to her friend. Chrissy smiled and Kevin nodded.

"I believe we met earlier this week?" Kevin asked. Chrissy nodded and Kevin sighed in relief. "One down, sixty to go. So how long have you been here, Chrissy?"

"All my life, like Elnora," Chrissy glanced over at her friend. "We grew up together."

"Ah … you're besties," Kevin said, leaning back to sit on the arm of the soft chair behind him. Elnora and Chrissy nodded together. "And do you teach 2nd grade too?" Kevin asked Chrissy.

"Yeah, though I'm not half as good as Elnora," she gently nudged Elnora's shoulder with her own. Elnora laughed.

"Not true at all, but thanks," Elnora said. Chrissy nodded conspiratorially toward Kevin, silently arguing with Elnora.

Kevin smiled. "Any chance you guys have some of that fresh Blue Whale Cove Coffee here?" Kevin looked over at the kitchenette.

"We surely do, along with a killer espresso machine," Elnora said. She turned and looked pointedly at Chrissy.

Chrissy's eyes widened, and then she nodded in understanding. "I'll show you," Chrissy said, leading Kevin over to the kitchenette and getting him all set up. She returned two minutes later, alone. "He likes you," she said casually, looking over at Elnora and then to Kevin.

"He's a nice guy; fun to talk to. I think he'll do well here," Elnora said, smiling as Kevin returned with his coffee. "Good stuff?" she asked, indicating the coffee. Kevin took a sip and nodded.

"Very good stuff," Kevin took another, longer sip and looked around the room. "So this is where you guys hide between classes?" He nodded appreciatively.

"When we can," Elnora said, taking a seat. "You're welcome to join us," Elnora suggested and Chrissy nodded, sitting down next to Elnora.

"Thank you. I have to admit that I'm still trying to get my bearings in the classroom with the lessons and all, so I'll probably be skipping breaks for awhile longer, but it's good to know you'll be waiting here when I'm ready," Kevin smiled at both of them.

"Do you need any help?" Elnora asked. "I mean, I'll admit that fourth grade isn't my specialty, but still--if you need help getting set up …" she dropped off the rest of the sentence and waited.

Kevin smiled. "Sometimes I wonder if fourth grade is really my specialty," the three of them laughed lightly. "Luckily I'm fairly experienced, so it's just a matter of getting oriented in Misty's classroom. I don't want to really change anything, especially this late in the year, so I'm just sorting out what's happening so I can be the most effective."

"Understood," Elnora said. "Speaking of which, it's about time to get back," Elnora pushed herself forward and stood.

"Didn't we *just* sit down?" Chrissy groaned, leaning forward to stand up as well.

"Of course!" Elnora gently patted her friend on the back.

Kevin drained the last of his coffee and placed the mug in the sink.

"Here we go again," Kevin said, winking at them before pulling open the door and holding it open. They thanked him, and then they all went to their separate classrooms.

CHAPTER 12

Elnora woke up at 7:00 am on Saturday morning, a not entirely unusual occurrence. She decided to head down to the beach for an early morning walk, and quickly put on her sweats and hiking shoes before heading outside.

The town was quiet and sleepy, the feeling all the more heightened by a thick blanket of dense fog. Elnora wasn't certain if it was the sort of fog that would burn off by 11:00 am, or the sort that would linger for the whole day, but she was hopeful that it was short-lived. She liked occasional, early-morning fogs, they created an almost romantic feeling in the small, coastal town. But an early-morning fog that burned off before lunch, revealing beautiful blue skies and a warm sun, was her absolute favorite.

Elnora crossed a largely-deserted Main Street and soon thereafter stepped onto the sand of the beach. She couldn't see the waves through the fog, and so she kept her eyes on the sand beneath her feet as she moved west, turning north as soon as she found the harder, wetter sand. She decided that this was one day it would be prudent to keep her eyes down on the ground, because even then she wasn't entirely sure she would spot the incoming tide more than a couple seconds before it hit her feet.

An hour and a half after she had walked out of the front door of her home, Elnora stood in front of it again. She placed the key in the lock, opened the door and stepped inside, kicking her shoes off in the entryway. The house felt almost hot after the cool dampness outside, and Elnora immediately stripped off her sweatshirt before heading to the bathroom for a hot shower.

By the time Elnora was dressed, the fog had already begun to burn off and blue skies and sunshine were peaking through. Elnora walked into her kitchen and whipped up a single serving of eggs benedict, with smoked salmon instead of ham, and then sat down at her table to eat breakfast and enjoy the ever-improving view out her back window. When she had used the last bit of english muffin to wipe up the last blob of hollandaise sauce, Elnora took her dishes to the sink, washed them and placed them in the dish rack, and then moved into her living room to read. She had been reading for fifteen minutes when her phone rang. She glanced at the screen and smiled, answering the call and putting the phone to her ear.

"Hi Chrissy."

"Hi!" Chrissy answered. "We're still on for today, right?"

"Yep, I'll pick you up at 11:30," Elnora confirmed.

"Actually, can we make it noon?" Chrissy asked, her voice sounding apologetic. "I'm running a little behind." Elnora laughed.

"On a Saturday morning? When did you wake up?" Elnora asked.

"Early," Chrissy said convincingly. "For me, anyway."

"So like twenty minutes ago?"

"No," Chrissy sounded offended. "It was like … thirty, maybe thirty-five minutes ago." Elnora laughed again.

"It's okay, I can give you the extra half hour," Elnora said.

"Thanks--see you soon!" Chrissy ended the call. Elnora set her phone down beside her and returned to her book, smiling and shaking her head.

"What are you doing?" Elnora called out the passenger car window at Chrissy, who had locked her front door, turned toward the car, paused, raised a "wait" finger toward Elnora, turned back to her front door, and was now unlocking it again.

"Hang on," Chrissy called back over her shoulder, just before disappearing inside her house. She returned a few moments later, a large blue bag in her hand. She relocked her front door and came out to the car, pulling open the passenger door and getting in. "I forgot my reusable bags," she explained as she pulled her seat belt around her body and secured it. She pushed the blue bag over their shoulders between them and into the backseat.

"Ah, I see," Elnora said, glancing over her left shoulder before pulling away from the curb. "Ready now?" Elnora asked, teasing her friend. Ever since they were young, Elnora was always the first one ready to go anywhere--and she was often extra early--while Chrissy was always running behind, scrambling to make sure she had everything she needed. When Chrissy told Elnora they would meet up at a certain time, Elnora always added a half hour. And so it was no real surprise that it was 12:45 before they were finally leaving Chrissy's house.

"Yes, I'm ready to go," Chrissy said, rolling her eyes and sighing in faux exasperation.

"Good. Here we go."

"Oh my gosh, I'm so glad that week is over," Chrissy laid her head back against the headrest and closed her eyes.

"A bit rough, huh?" Elnora asked, turning onto Cedar Street and then promptly stopping to let a man and his dog cross the street in front of them. As soon as feet and paws hit sidewalk, Elnora released the brake and continued to creep along Cedar Street.

"Not a bit rough," Chrissy groaned, "Really, really rough. Every single period there was some new challenge--the sorts I normally have once every couple weeks. It was totally crazy!"

"I'm sorry to hear that," Elnora glanced over at her friend, pulling gently to a stop at the intersection with Main Street. "Anything I can help with?"

Chrissy shrugged. "I don't know," Chrissy said glumly. "I honestly don't feel like it's anything new that I haven't dealt with before or that I don't know how to handle. It's just a lot all at once, and it's exhausting."

"I understand," Elnora said, pulling out onto Main Street and heading south. Chrissy looked over at her, a question in her eyes.

"Do you? Really?" Chrissy asked earnestly. "I mean, I know that you've never had a perfect class, where every student always does what you ask them to do or what they need to do, but you never seem to get at all stressed or anxious about it, whereas I feel stressed or anxious *all the time*," Chrissy heavily emphasized the last three words. Elnora looked over at her friend, Chrissy's eyes imploring her for help.

"The truth?" Elnora asked, turning her eyes back to

the road, and Chrissy nodded. "It's challenging," Elnora admitted, shrugging her shoulders to signify that there was no point denying it. Chrissy scoffed. "Okay, it's incredibly challenging, some days and some weeks more so than others. But I knew that coming into teaching, and it's honestly one of the things I love most about teaching," Elnora smiled. Chrissy frowned. "I'm not trying to affect a change wherein kids are perfectly well-behaved all the time and never have any difficulties that they need help with. We need kids who are bull-headed and free-thinkers so that they grow up into adults who are brave enough to change the world. Sometimes that helps, by the way," Elnora held up her finger to make a point. "Instead of complaining about how ... Suzy is always speaking out loudly and interrupting during class, I think about how she would be a good orator--maybe a politician. And instead of worrying over the fact that Cameron just can't handle corrections or confrontations without turning into a puddle of tears, I think about how his sensitivity and kindness will help him bolster his friends' moods whenever they're struggling with some particularly difficult challenges in their lives." Elnora looked over at Chrissy, who was listening carefully. "It also helps to remember all the kids you've helped in the past. Remember Ricky? He couldn't read at all--but he made enough of the right sounds that he had convinced every other teacher before you that he could read and he just had a terrible stutter. You were the one who figured out that he couldn't really read at all, and you were the one who spent tens of hours with him every month, helping him to practice and master his phonics. You didn't even ask me for help on that one, you figured it out on your own!" Elnora looked over again to see her friend beaming. "And by the time the year was out, Ricky was one of the strongest readers in your class.

He's still getting reading awards every year, and he's in fifth grade now!" Chrissy nodded.

"He did amazing," Chrissy conceded.

"*You* did amazing too," Elnora corrected her friend.

"Okay, so I do love those parts too, and they're definitely why I decided to become a teacher," Chrissy relaxed and sighed. "But it's just that when the challenges and difficulties pile up all at once, it's stressful and really hard to see through to the other side."

"And *that's* why I go for walks all the time," Elnora said. "Exercise helps to release endorphins, and endorphins make you happy," they both giggled as Elnora mimicked the line from *Legally Blonde*. "Really though, you should try it. I bet you'd notice a difference."

"I dunno," Chrissy said uncertainly. "I'm so tired when the school day is over, it's just easy to go home, handle any 'homework' I need to handle, eat some food, watch my shows and go to bed."

"Well that's the thing. My legs and feet might be tired after my walks, but I always feel more energized when I get back home. I get more done in less time, and I sleep better at night. Which also helps to minimize stress and anxiety," Elnora added in her best know-it-all voice. Chrissy scoffed again.

"Great, now you sound like my mom."

"She is a wise woman," Elnora offered helpfully.

"Yes, I know," Chrissy agreed. "And you are too," she smiled over at her friend. They drove on in silence for another fifteen minutes, arriving at the Tillamook Fred Meyer shortly after 1:00 pm. Chrissy grabbed her reusable bags and they headed into the huge store, wandering down separate aisles with their separate carts, but crossing paths every few minutes. An hour later, pushing carts filled with various household and grocery items, they worked their way through neighboring checkout lines and then walked out into the parking lot and over to Elnora's car. Elnora popped the trunk and they loaded their purchases inside, not bothering to separate them since Elnora's bags were the store's generic plastic ones next to Chrissy's colorful reusable bags. After placing the last bag in the trunk, Chrissy grabbed both carts and pushed them over to the return receptacle while Elnora closed the trunk and unlocked the driver's door. She had just sat down and unlocked the passenger door when Chrissy grabbed the passenger door handle, pulling the door open and sliding in. They both pulled their seatbelts out and secured them, and Elnora started the car.

"Ice cream?" Elnora looked over at Chrissy.

"Ice cream," Chrissy nodded.

They drove a half mile north and pulled into the parking lot for the Tillamook Cheese Factory. Elnora didn't even bother driving up and down the first few parking aisles, which were always pretty packed, but rather drove straight back onto the gravel part of the lot and pulled into the first available spot. She shut off the engine and they both stepped out onto the gravel. Elnora locked the car and they headed toward the main entrance.

"Watch out," Chrissy said, placing a hand on Elnora's arm just before Elnora stepped out to cross the road. A car drove by slowly, the driver clearly lost as they were going towards the delivery area rather than the parking area. Chrissy dropped her arm off Elnora's and they crossed the road, walking up to and through the fancy new front doors of the factory. The lobby opened before them, with a huge staircase on the right leading up to the second floor and the self-guided factory tour. Chrissy and Elnora stayed to the left, around the corner into the food area and the ice-cream line. The line was one of the longer ones they had seen; there were roughly fifty people in front of them. They weren't even slightly concerned, as the line was often long but it always moved quickly. Five minutes later, Elnora stepped up to pay for her single scoop and then moved to the right to place her flavor order, choosing mint chocolate chip, followed by Chrissy, who stepped up to pay for her single scoop and moved to the right to place her flavor order, also choosing mint chocolate chip. They each grabbed two napkins from the dispenser and then walked toward the indoor dining area, through the door and out to the outdoor dining area. They found two spots next to each other on a long wooden bench and sat down, both of them working to keep their ice cream from dripping down their cones and onto their hands.

"I went over to Misty's last night and met Sophia Rose," Chrissy said, capturing a drip that had made its way down to her thumb. "She's really adorable."

"I know, I had a hard time giving her back when I went by on Wednesday night," Elnora said, taking a small bite off the top of her ice cream.

"It's kind of weird, and I know that it's not easy to have a baby or adjust to the new schedule afterwards, plus you want to spend as much time with them as you can, but still I think it's kind of weird that she's going to be out for three whole months."

"I know," Elnora agreed. "It seems like such a long time. On the other hand, at the end of the three months, when Misty has to leave her baby with a nanny and come back to work, I'm willing to bet she'll be talking about how it went by so fast and how she wishes it was a six-month maternity leave." Chrissy nodded and nibbled at the edge of her ice cream cone.

"Is she running a summer camp class?" Chrissy asked.

"That's what she told me she planned to do, but that was before she had Sophia. We'll see how it actually plays out when the time comes. I'm sure Kevin would happily continue to cover for her if asked," Elnora took a big bite of cone, enjoying the crunch.

"How do you think he's doing?" Chrissy asked. "Or maybe he's told you?" Elnora shook her head.

"No, we talked about other things. I assume he's doing fine, especially since they've placed him on provisional employment. Someone had to have watched him in the classroom and thought he was doing fine."

"He seems a little nervous."

"I think that's kind of normal--he's meeting so many new people all at once. Imagine what it would be like if you walked into a school down in Lincoln City." Chrissy shook her head and grunted. "Exactly. He probably just doesn't feel comfortable with crowds of new people. Can't really blame him," Elnora took another bite of her ice cream.

"Nope, I guess not," Chrissy licked her ice cream

"Did you know that Samantha Hiller was his aunt?" Elnora asked thoughtfully.

"What?" Chrissy asked.

"Yeah, he told me the other day that he used to come up and visit her all the time before she passed. That's how he knew about Blue Whale Cove--he'd been here often enough to fall in love with the place."

"Why didn't we ever see him? Or hear about him?" Chrissy's voice was suspicious, matching Elnora's own initial consternation.

"He says that they usually stayed indoors during his visits, baking, reading and playing board games, and that Samantha wasn't actually much of a gossip about personal things, despite appearances to the contrary."

"He came all the way to Blue Whale Cove, often, and never went outside in town or along the beach?" Chrissy asked skeptically, licking away some ice cream that was dripping down her cone.

"He didn't say never. Actually, he said he occasionally went out for walks while Samantha was napping."

"Still, it sounds kind of weird," Chrissy raised her eyebrows and looked over at her friend. "I remember that Samantha loved to gossip--remember she would tell and retell the story of how her father earned his Purple Heart?" Elnora nodded, smiling. "It was payment for her baked goods--she'd bring you her incredible apple pie and you listened to her stories and then shared some of your own."

"That's how I remember her too," Elnora took another bite of her ice cream cone, chewing the soft, sweet treat. "She was so kind and friendly, and sort of funny too."

Chrissy nodded. "Doesn't really match up to someone who kept secrets," she said matter-of-factly.

Elnora shrugged. "True. But then I guess anyone could have some secrets that they don't share--even if they share everything else." Chrissy glanced over at her friend, but Elnora missed the surprised look on her face as she glanced down at her ice cream. They both fell silent, finishing up the last of their ice creams, and Elnora knew they were thinking the same thing.

What else didn't they know about Blue Whale Cove?

CHAPTER 13

The itch was back--a deep, driving need that was impossible to ignore.

It seemed to be coming more often and more urgently these days.

It was accompanied, as it always was, by the image of a single object.

That image pervaded their every waking thought; it even invaded their dreams.

Fortunately, they had long since learned that there was one way to scratch it.

They had to satisfy that need.

They had been mostly lucky so far, but last time carelessness had alerted others prematurely.

They couldn't risk another incident like that.

They had to be careful.

They had to plan and choose their every motion and moment wisely.

They couldn't wait to hold the object in their hands, and then put it where they would always be able to find it.

The object was perfect.

It was exactly what they needed to satisfy the itch.

CHAPTER 14

Right around 4:30 pm on Saturday, March 10th, Ms. Anastasia Tasken left her little blue house on Pine Street to drive down to Tillamook and have dinner with her sister, which was something they did every Saturday afternoon. Like many of the other houses on the street, Anastasia's house was neither large nor small, but a rather comfortable, eighteen hundred square foot home set on a nice-sized lot. Anastasia liked tasteful landscaping that provided privacy, but she was not at all a gardener, so she hired someone to come out every couple of weeks to mow her lawns, weed and take care of various other gardening tasks. The result was a beautiful front and back yard which each boasted many native plants that tended to grow tall and wide. Anastasia loved the sort of private sanctuary the plants created, especially since it meant that she could forego window coverings on many of her windows and still maintain privacy.

Anastasia pulled her house key out of her large, leather

handbag, locked her front door, got into the small car parked in the driveway, and drove off down the street.

Roughly ten minutes later, Anastasia's neighbor directly across the street, Mr. Gregory Chift, got up from the rocker on his front porch, where he had a perfect view across the entire front of Anastasia's house. He walked across his long, covered porch and went inside his own house, his four decaf coffees having finally made their way through his system.

As soon as Gregory disappeared into his house, a shadow passed through Anastasia's front garden, moved quietly through the gate on the north side of the house and into the backyard, and gently pushed up the window that opened into her bedroom. The window frame sat slightly crooked in the wall, with a long crack running along the top of it. Years of moisture had seeped into the wood around the frame, forcing the crack to widen and the window to sit at its strange angle. As a result, the window could be closed with some force, but it would not latch, something Anastasia didn't worry about in her small, safe town. The shadow moved in through the open window and into Anastasia's bedroom.

Roughly two minutes later, the shadow exited through the window, pushing it down firmly but gently. The window got stuck halfway down and the force used to close it was accordingly increased, causing the window to bang loudly as it finally came down. The small, elderly and nearly blind cat sleeping on the pillow at the head of Anastasia's bed jumped in surprise, scrambling to leave the bed for the comfort of the hall closet, and knocking into a small, latched wooden box on the nightstand as it went. The wooden box teetered on the edge of the nightstand for one moment before tumbling to the ground, coming to a rest precisely where Anastasia placed her slippers each night.

The shadow moved silently through the gate on the north

side of Anastasia's house, back through her front garden, and disappeared down the street.

Mere moments later, Gregory came out his front door and returned to the rocking chair on his front porch, where he spent the vast majority of his time--rocking, reading, sipping coffee and watching cars and people.

Two hours after she had left, Anastasia turned her car into her driveway, put it in park, got out and walked up to her front door. She carefully closed and locked the door behind her and then spent fifteen minutes looking for her beloved cat, Buttercup. She normally found Buttercup sleeping on her pillow whenever she returned home, but today her bed was empty. It was odd enough that Anastasia felt she should locate the cat and ensure she was okay. She was relieved when she finally discovered that Buttercup was fine, and sleeping peacefully in the hallway closet.

Happy in the knowledge that her elderly and health-challenged cat was okay, Anastasia moved into her bedroom and began to prepare for bed (she was an early-to-bed, early-to-rise woman, she always had been--even forty years ago when she was in her twenties). As she sat on her bed to remove her stockings, she noticed the small, wooden box on the floor but didn't think much of it; Buttercup was nearly blind and often knocked things over as she moved about the house. As Anastasia lifted the box back onto the nightstand, however, she knew something was wrong. The box was far too light. She held the box up to her face and pushed and slid the latch so that the box would open--revealing an empty interior. Even as her heart began to beat harder, Anastasia immediately looked to the floor, getting down onto her knees to search under the bed. Satisfied nothing was there, she stood and searched the top of the nightstand, behind the nightstand, and inside the nightstand (even though the drawer had been closed and Buttercup certainly couldn't have done that). She threw back the sheets on her bed, pushed her hand gently between the mattress and the frame, and even grabbed the flashlight she kept in her nightstand drawer and checked everywhere in the bedroom she could think of.

Finally, after having satisfied herself that she had thoroughly searched her bedroom, that the wooden box couldn't unlatch and then relatch itself, and that she was absolutely certain the box had been full before she had left for her sister's house (since she had opened it and checked it herself that afternoon for the first time in a very, very long time), Anastasia came to the only conclusion she could: her grandfather's gold enamel pocket watch, with the beautiful inlaid purple violet on the front, had been stolen.

CHAPTER 15

Elnora gazed out once more at the open ocean views and then turned back to the trail, following it as it curved to the north and deeper into the forest. Elnora welcomed the cooler air, breathing deeply and relaxing her mind. She was used to walking off persistent, stressful thoughts on this hike, in fact it was one of the greatest benefits of this hike--the mild challenges, the temperature changes and the views tended to pull her out of unconstructive thoughts and allow her to relax and focus on problem-solving. But in all her years of hiking this trail, she had never struggled to relax her mind for more than the first quarter of the hike--and certainly not more than a full half of the hike. What was most puzzling to her was the recognition that she wasn't dealing with a big problem, or something else that would be the source of major stress. It was just a small doubt that was festering in the back of her mind, causing just enough confusion to make her feel slightly lost.

Elnora had spoken with Kevin for long enough on Thursday to be certain that he had dropped his guard and been completely open with her. Their conversations were real and raw, not the sort of thing that could be easily faked. Elnora had always been able to read people--the good, the bad and everywhere in between. It was an instinct she had always trusted and one that had never let her down. But now she wasn't entirely sure, and that bothered her.

She knew that if she simply confronted Kevin with her doubts, he would address them--he seemed to be honest and kind. But for some reason, she couldn't find the courage to do this simple thing. A voice in the back of her mind told her that it was because she was shy, and that the truth was that she liked Kevin. She silenced the voice immediately, but it pushed back in, trying to convince her that it was normal to resist learning about the faults of someone you liked.

With another deep breath that left her like a sigh, Elnora tried yet again to push doubts of Kevin from her mind. She stepped onto and crossed over a wooden walkway, smiling at the young boy who was trying desperately to "accidentally" step down into the mud in order to try out his apparently brand-new hiking boots. His mother kept gently urging him ahead, impressively thwarting his attempts to step into the mud without directly telling him "no" or "stop." Elnora hopped over the small mud puddle at the end of the walkway and continued on, walking carefully around an assortment of rocks and tree roots. Her mind wandered to Samantha Hiller.

While it was certainly true that Blue Whale Cove felt small enough for everyone to know everyone else, it was also true that residents knew certain people better than others. Elnora felt that while she had known Samantha Hiller, she hadn't known her as well as she had known other residents in Blue Whale Cove. To put it another way--she felt that she knew *about* Samantha more than she *knew* her.

Samantha had been a petite woman, maybe 5'4", and sturdily-built, though Elnora remembered that she had slowly lost weight as she got older, achieving a much more slender build by the time she passed. She hadn't been that old when she passed on--perhaps her mid-sixties. Elnora remembered how shocked and saddened the town had felt for weeks after Samantha's passing, and it was in that way that Samantha had been everyone's family. Samantha had a round, friendly face with small, dark brown eyes and she usually wore a broad smile, especially when she was sharing her delicious homemade treats. This is where Elnora's memory was crystal clear. She remembered perfectly how much Samantha loved to give and receive news whenever she dropped off treats, which she did often.

Elnora remembered sitting on the couch in her parent's house at eleven years old, Samantha sitting on the big comfy chair across from her, and listening with wide eyes to the stories Samantha had to share. They seemed wonderfully exciting to her, though her mother kept coming by and interrupting Samanatha with various suggestions--all of which seemed to involve Samantha going home. Samantha brushed away these suggestions, saying that she wasn't tired yet, she wasn't worried about returning home in the dark, she had eaten dinner before she came and so forth. Elnora was glad Samantha didn't want to leave and her mother didn't force Samantha to leave, because she wanted to hear everything Samantha had to say. She talked about interesting things, like how little Billy down the street had sprained his ankle when he climbed onto the roof of the shed in his backyard and then jumped from it, spreading his wings like a bird, and how Johnny Stanberg was madly in love with Fiona Ackerman, and would surely be proposing to her any day now. Then, when Samantha was done sharing her stories, she sat and listened to whatever Elnora had to say, asking questions and becoming excited when Elnora knew the answers. It made Elnora feel important and special.

Samantha stopped by Elnora's parent's house every few months or so, always with something that smelled incredible and tasted even better, and always visiting for awhile. Now that Elnora thought about it, Samantha did seem to visit less and less frequently in the three years before she passed. While she wasn't that old at the time, Samantha's passing had always been attributed to natural causes--likely because there was no other explanation.

Elnora paused at a bend in the trail, pulled out her cold water bottle and took a long drink. She had passed quite a few hikers on her way out to the point, but now that she herself was returning she found that the trail was almost deserted. A dense fog that had been sitting on the western horizon had since crept slowly toward the coast, and Elnora knew that it would continue creeping east until it reached between ten to thirty miles inland. Though the morning had started as warm and sunny, it would be a cool and damp afternoon and evening.

Elnora took another sip of cool water and then returned the bottle to her backpack and her backpack to her back. Her stomach gurgled quietly and she glanced down at her watch. It was 11:42 am, if she hustled back to her car she should make it to the Cafe well before Jeffrey changed the sign. She continued slowly along the trail, and recognized the distant, muffled sound of an approaching hiker. All at once, a man appeared around a curve in the trail about fifty yards ahead of Elnora, and something about him made Elnora stop. From this distance, the man looked a lot like Kevin, tall with dark brown hair, but something about the way he was walking made Elnora unsure whether it was him. Even if it was Kevin, Elnora wasn't sure she wanted to run into him--the voice in the back of her mind told her it was bashfulness, but she argued it was confusion and doubt.

The man was looking all around him, not as though he were enjoying the view and the scenery, but rather as though he were checking to make sure no one was watching him. Impulsively, Elnora stepped to the side of the trail and behind a large tree, just as the man turned and looked her way. After what seemed an eternity, Elnora peered around the tree trunk and down the trail. The man looked around him one final time, pulled his backpack up higher on his back, and stepped off the trail and into the bushes, walking quickly but lightly among the ferns that carpeted the forest floor. Elnora remained behind the tree until well after the sound of the man's footsteps had faded away, and then she stepped back onto the trail. She walked slowly forward along the trail, her heart pounding in her chest as though she expected a surprise to jump out at her at any moment. When she came to the spot where the man had gone off the trail, Elnora looked down into the forest but saw nothing.

She felt uncomfortable remaining in the area, not knowing what the man was doing or how long he would be, so she picked up her pace as she continued along the trail toward the parking lot. When she came up the last rise to the nearly empty parking lot, she spotted the old 1980's Toyota station wagon, and her breath caught in her throat. She was now certain that the man on the trail had been Kevin, because she hadn't passed him at any other point. The voice in the back of her mind argued that he could've taken the southern trail to the beach or the northern trail, but even the voice sounded weak and uncertain to her. Elnora on the other hand felt absolutely certain it had been Kevin she had seen, stepping off the trail and into the forest. But what had he been doing? She couldn't imagine why anyone would want to leave the trail and go traipsing through the woods at Cape Lookout--especially since it was a relatively narrow peninsula with sheer drop offs all along the way.

Elnora's heart continued to pound as she moved over to her car, opened the trunk and dumped her backpack in. She quickly moved around to the driver's door, got in, started the engine, and drove out of the lot and north towards home, all the while feeling like she was the guilty one. She also felt a deep disappointment, because for the first time ever, her hike hadn't worked as well at calming her mind as it normally did.

CHAPTER 16

As she had predicted, Elnora arrived at the Cafe well before closing time, surprising Jeffrey when she walked in and sat down at the counter. He seemed to sense that she was preoccupied, so he placed her glass of ice water in front of her and went off to the kitchen to place her order. Elnora turned on her stool, grateful for the lunch crowd and the attendant noise to distract her from her thoughts.

The Cafe wasn't loaded to capacity, but it certainly wasn't as empty as it normally was when Elnora stopped by for her late Sunday lunches. By the time she usually made it by, the crowd had dwindled so significantly that Jeffrey sent his extra wait staff home and took care of the final few customers himself. Today, even with three other waiters manning the booths and counter, Jeffrey had his hands full waiting tables and ensuring orders were placed and delivered on time. Nearly all the booths were in use, along with a little less than half the stools at the counter. Elnora saw a sea of happy, largely unfamiliar faces--tourists stopping for a bite to eat in the cute local cafe of a quaint, coastal town. Scanning the booths, her eyes came to rest on a solitary diner, sitting alone in the largest corner booth, reading a dog-eared book and slowly sipping spoonfuls of soup. Elnora grabbed her water glass and got up, motioned to Jeffrey to indicate that she was moving, and walked over to the corner booth.

"Hi Ruth," Elnora said gently. The older woman looked up from her book and smiled warmly at Elnora. Ruth Wickerd was seventy-eight years old, and easily one of the nicest women that Elnora had ever met. Ruth had married very well, to a husband who ran one of the largest paper mills in Oregon, and she had retired from her career as a hairdresser at the comfortable age of fifty. She had only retired, however, in order to help others. She helped whenever and wherever she could, with fundraisers at the schools, fire station or library, with the homeless shelter down in Lincoln City, and even with tutoring. Her husband retired when he was sixty-five, and preferred to spend his time in front of the television at home, but Ruth still preferred her more active social life. Over the years she had grown a little more stooped when she stood and walked, a little slower in her speech and perhaps a little less precise with her writing, but she still loved to help. Elnora realized she hadn't seen her in over a month, and was happy to have a moment to catch up with her.

"Elnora, how lovely to see you, dear!" Ruth closed her book and placed it on the table beside her soup.

"I don't want to interrupt your reading, but I was wondering if I may join you?"

"Of course, please!" Ruth waved an arthritic hand at the booth across from her, and Elnora sank onto the soft vinyl. "I can read any time, but I'd much rather spend time enjoying your company." Jeffrey appeared suddenly, placing Elnora's tuna melt in front of her before rushing off again. Elnora unrolled her napkin, placing it on her lap and picking up the fork and knife to cut a bite of her sandwich.

"I haven't seen you in awhile, how have you been?" Elnora asked, putting the food into her mouth and chewing.

"Fine, fine," Ruth smiled, revealing loose dentures. She lifted her glass of iced tea to her lips and drank slowly. "I've been spending lots of time with Suzy, and that's nice," Ruth put her glass down. "We're knitting hats for cancer patients, it gives us lots of time to chit chat." Ruth smiled.

"That's very lovely of you both. And Suzy, how is she doing?" Elnora asked cautiously.

"Not very well," Ruth admitted, her eyes sad. "This whole insurance business is such a … well it's a bit of a nightmare, really." Ruth sat back, leaning back against the booth and sighing.

"What's wrong?" Elnora asked. The last she had heard, the insurance adjuster was supposed to have come out at the end of the week to file his report, and since it all seemed fairly straight-forward, she assumed Suzy would have her check within a month.

"The insurance adjuster came out on Thursday, to gather information for the claim," Ruth paused and sipped more soup. Elnora forced herself to cut another bite of sandwich and eat it. "And apparently, Suzy's policy dictates that when checking on the damage or theft of any insured item, they verify the condition of all other insured items." Elnora nodded, it made sense. "Suzy has seven items insured with them," Ruth paused again, taking another sip of iced tea. "She has such nice things, my Suzy does," Ruth stopped, pride for her successful daughter showing plainly in her eyes.

"So they checked the other items?" Elnora said gently. Ruth nodded, her face darkening again.

"They asked to see the other six items," Ruth said, and Elnora waited patiently for the rest of the sentence. "But Suzy could only find three of them," Ruth shook her head. Elnora wrinkled her forehead in confusion. "She cannot find her amethyst pressed glass lamp from the Boston & Sandwich Glass company, her antique milk glass Easter eggs or her Lalique eucalyptus flacon." Ruth pronounced each word smoothly and easily, and Elnora suspected that she had practiced a lot--it was clear that she had been telling this news to many others.

"What do you mean? Has she lost them?" Ruth shook her head again, raising sad eyes to meet Elnora's.

"She isn't sure," Ruth said slowly, "But she thinks they might also have been taken. So strange, too. I mean, they were pretty, to be sure, but they weren't terribly valuable. Not nearly as valuable as the Fabergé pendant, of course. She didn't even keep them out on open display--only so much room you know--so she kept them in a little trunk in her bedroom. I just cannot figure who would want to take them, and why. They wouldn't get that much for them, even if they did sell them. But for Suzy, the problem is that she doesn't know when they were taken, if indeed they were, and that doesn't make the insurance company too happy," Ruth sighed."

"Oh no," Elnora said, with real feeling. Ruth nodded. "So what, they won't pay to make her whole?"

"They haven't said that. But what was supposed to be a simple claim has turned into a complete nightmare. Suzy has to file police reports for all the missing items, upgrade her home security system, and jump through a bunch of other hoops. It's exhausting just to think about," Ruth said, sipping more of her soup. Elnora nodded.

"I'm so sorry," Elnora said, reaching out and putting her hand on Ruth's arm. She wanted to change the subject, but could only think of one thing. "Did you know that Samantha Hiller had a nephew who visited her regularly?" Ruth's expression changed, from concern and sadness to confusion.

"Samantha?" Ruth frowned, thinking hard. "I know she had a brother who lived in Beaverton. I don't remember regular visits from family, but then again, we weren't terribly close." Ruth leaned forward a little, and placed her hand near her mouth, as though to tell a secret, "I'm an old fuddy-duddy, you know, and Samantha was half a generation younger," she leaned back again, her eyes twinkling. "Why do you ask, dear?" Ruth reached out and grabbed her iced tea again, taking a long drink.

"Her nephew has taken a job at the school," Elnora said casually. Ruth's eyes brightened.

"Oh really? Well that's lovely," Ruth placed her glass back on the table and picked up her soup bowl so she could get the last bits. Elnora followed her lead and worked on her sandwich, which was growing cooler by the minute. When the conversation started up again, it was just social talk--about the weather, Elnora's job, and Ruth's health. Elnora could tell that Ruth was becoming tired, and she therefore wasn't at all surprised when Ruth politely excused herself shortly thereafter. Elnora offered to drive Ruth home, but Ruth smiled and indicated out the window, where Suzy was waiting with her Lexus. Ruth explained that Suzy had needed to run an errand down in Tillamook, but had promised to return on time to take her home. And, Ruth added with a wide smile, Suzy always kept her promises. Elnora agreed that was true, and she helped Ruth down the steps of the Cafe and to the car. She greeted Suzy briefly, thanked Ruth for the lovely company, and gently closed the car door, watching as they moved smoothly away. Her chat with Ruth had done what her hike had failed to do--make her feel calmer.

CHAPTER 17

Elnora parked her car in her driveway and then walked down the street to Chrissy's house. This time she had to wait a couple of minutes before Chrissy opened the door--though she heard Chrissy holler "Coming!" from the kitchen and then move into the hallway and bedroom area. By the time Chrissy opened the door, Elnora had a quizzical look on her face.

"What?" Chrissy asked, closing the door gently after her friend.

"You ran from the kitchen to the hallway and bedroom area, without stopping to open the door along the way," Elnora said by way of explanation. Chrissy made an embarrassed face.

"I didn't have a shirt on, so I ran to grab one," she looked down and smoothed her t-shirt, a white one with small, embroidered yellow daisies around the collar. Elnora's quizzical look deepened.

"And why were you shirtless?" Elnora inquired, following Chrissy into the kitchen. For once, the table was set for tea, and the teapot was heating on the stove. Elnora was impressed.

"I spilled chocolate on my other one," Chrissy explained, as though it were a perfectly normal event, "And I took it off to soak it," she pointed toward the bathroom, "But I hadn't finished setting out the tea things, so I didn't go into the bedroom right away for a new shirt." Chrissy sounded like a child who was trying to explain to their mother why they were home an hour later than they were supposed to be.

"Chocolate?" Elnora said, glancing around the table. Her eyes alighted on a small rectangle, the wrapping partially pulled away. She picked up the bar, noting that it was dark chocolate with orange peels.

"Yes, chocolate," Chrissy said, knowing no further explanation was necessary. "Try some," she encouraged Elnora, who had already begun to peel back the wrapping. Elnora broke off a small square and placed it into her mouth. "Good, isn't it? I grabbed it at Fred Meyer yesterday."

"It's very good," Elnora agreed, placing the chocolate bar back on the table and having a seat.

"So?" Chrissy asked, pulling the whistling teapot off the stove and shutting it off. "What's the rumor mill got today?" She placed the teapot on the stone trivet and sat down across from Elnora.

"Nothing, actually," Elnora pulled a chamomile tea from the tea caddy and pushed it back toward Chrissy. Chrissy raised her eyebrows as she selected an orange spice tea and pushed the caddy back into the center of the table. Elnora opened her mouth to tell Chrissy about Kevin disappearing into the woods on the Cape Lookout trail and then closed it again. She wasn't sure she wanted to get into it, especially since Chrissy would only deepen her doubt and confusion. The voice in the back of her mind teased that it was because she really liked him and she shrugged it away.

"Nothing?" Chrissy's voice was skeptical.

"Well, I didn't connect with the rumor mill today," Elnora explained, ripping open her tea package and placing her tea bag in her mug. "I got to the cafe early and caught Ruth Wickerd."

Chrissy smiled. "I haven't seen Ruth in forever!" Chrissy gushed.

"I hadn't either," Elnora agreed.

"How is she?"

"She's doing well. She and Suzy are knitting hats for some charity, of course," Elnora said, pouring hot water into her mug.

"Of course," Chrissy said, opening her tea package and placing her tea bag in her mug.

"She's worried about Suzy," Elnora said, dipping her spoon into the honey jar and twirling it carefully before moving it over to her mug.

"I'm sure," Chrissy responded, dipping her own spoon into the honey jar. "Biscuits?" she asked, standing up. Elnora shook her head. Chrissy shrugged and grabbed the tin out of the cabinet anyway.

"Well it seems there's a little trouble with the insurance," Elnora explained, stirring her tea and then taking a tiny sip. "I guess Suzy had a few other items insured through the same company, less valuable ones than the pendant but valuable nonetheless, and several of them are missing." Chrissy coughed, spewing tiny cookie crumbs on the table before her. "Are you alright?" Elnora asked, looking around for a glass for water. Chrissy nodded, coughing once more and then clearing her throat.

"Cookie down the wrong pipe," Chrissy said hoarsely, standing and grabbing her water glass by the sink. She took a long sip. "What do you mean, missing?" she asked, returning to the table.

"Well that's the tricky part--Suzy isn't sure if they're just 'missing' missing, or if they might have also been taken," Elnora shrugged again. "But apparently it's messing up her insurance claim and creating a bit of a nightmare." Elnora took another tiny sip of tea.

"I hate insurance companies," Chrissy said. Elnora nodded.

"I don't suppose anyone really loves them. That is, until they come in really handy," Elnora said, and Chrissy nodded. "I'm sure it'll be alright in the end," Elnora added. "It just doesn't look like it'll be a smooth, easy claim, like they had hoped it would be. I'm sure Suzy just wants it to be over with so she can go on with her life, forget about it."

Chrissy nodded. "Me too." Elnora looked up at her friend, caught the look of deep thought on her face.

"I'm sure you'll be fine," Elnora said again, patting Chrissy's arm. "No need to worry." Chrissy smiled up at her friend's face. "Anyway, let's talk about something else," Elnora tapped the table with her open palm, signaling a change of subject.

The two friends drank tea and chatted for another two hours before Elnora finally headed for home, saying she had to get her laundry done before dinner time or she wouldn't get it done at all. Chrissy smiled and waved her friend off, before closing the door behind her. Elnora heard the deadbolt slide into place and smiled, walking down the driveway to the sidewalk and back down the street to her home.

CHAPTER 18

Elnora sat at her desk and admired her students. They were all sitting quietly in their chairs, reading. Reading time was usually the quietest part of her entire teaching day, but today was exceptionally quiet. It was somewhat unusual for any day, but particularly unusual for a Monday, when her students were coming off the weekend and whatever unusual sleep schedule, dietary oddities and extra screen arrangements they had experienced. It was simply one of those rare events when all of her students had received exactly what they needed over the weekend to have a wonderful Monday, and she was grateful for it.

As Elnora looked around at the individual faces, she was amused by the fact that she could guess the type of story some of her students were reading based upon the look on their faces. Molly looked perplexed and was chewing the end of her hair, so it was easy to guess that she was reading a story that had an element of suspense or mystery. Harrison's lips were curled up in the slightest hint of a smile; obviously his story was light and amusing. The look on Bentley's face was so intense that Elnora imagined he could burn a hole through the pages of his book; clearly he was reading about science, his favorite subject.

Elnora glanced up at the clock and noticed the time, frowning slightly. "Okay everyone," Elnora said quietly, watching her students' heads snap up. "I know you are all enjoying your reading very much, and you're all doing a wonderful job--I'm very proud of you," Elnora said, smiling warmly at her class. Several of her students smiled back at her. "But the bell for first recess is about to ring, so let's go ahead and clean up," Elnora had barely said the last word before the bell rang, startling a few of her students, who were trying to read the last bit of their page or story. The noise level in the room increased slightly as the students pushed back their chairs and moved to put away their books, chatting with one another. Elnora moved to the door and held it open for her students, who quietly filed into the hallway and toward the recess yard.

After pushing in a few chairs that had been neglected by their owners, Elnora stepped out into the hallway and walked down to the lounge. She pushed open the door and was surprised to see five solemn faces, gathered in the center of the room. It looked like she had interrupted a very serious discussion. Elnora stood in the doorway, almost uncertain about how to proceed.

"What is it?" Elnora asked, looking around. She noticed that neither Chrissy nor Kevin were in the room.

"There's been another burglary," Stan explained, his voice muted. Elnora raised her eyebrows in surprise and looked at the others, who nodded.

"What burglary?" Elnora asked, stepping fully into the room and allowing the door to close behind her.

"Anastasia Tasken's gold enamel pocket watch was stolen sometime on Saturday evening--while Anastasia was out visiting her sister," Bethany explained. Bethany taught third grade, and though she was a very good teacher and a very kind person, she and Elnora didn't spend much time together. Elnora shook her head sadly.

"She's sure it was stolen?" Elnora asked, hoping that there may have been some mistake. Stan nodded.

"She said that she had just checked it before she left for her sister's--on a whim. When she got home, the box was on the floor, latched, and she assumed Buttercup had just pushed it off the nightstand," Stan explained. "But when she picked it up, she could tell it was too light. And when she opened the box, it was empty. She searched everywhere for it, but it was definitely gone."

"That's awful," Elnora said. "But what about Gregory? He must've seen something." This time, it was Bethany who shook her head.

"He didn't see anything. He said he was on the front porch most of the afternoon--he remembers Anastasia leaving and returning. He just went inside once, for a couple minutes," Bethany said.

"So maybe the thief got in from the back, which is very unlikely," Stan said, and they all nodded. Anastasia's entire back yard was fenced in, and while it was not impossible for someone to have scaled the fence, it was almost impossible for their entry to have gone unnoticed, since all three connected yards contained large dogs who would not have remained quiet had their space been intruded upon. "What's more likely is that the thief was watching Greg, and made their move when he went indoors."

“That’s a tricky business,” Bethany argued. “How could they know how long Greg would be inside?” Stan shrugged.

“Perhaps they have been watching,” Stan offered, “You know, they scouted the house and neighborhood out first.” Elnora shivered involuntarily.

“But how would they even know that Anastasia had the pocket watch?” Bethany asked. “It’s not like she paraded it around town. She didn’t even keep it openly on display in her house.” The entire room fell silent. Everyone was thinking the same thing--the only way someone would’ve known about Anastasia’s watch is if they heard her, or someone else in town, talking about it. That meant that the thief wasn’t a random drifter, passing through town. More likely, they were a resident. Or related to a resident.

“Oh my gosh. Please don’t say anything to Chrissy,” Elnora suddenly broke the silence. She looked around at each of the five faces in the room, her eyes pleading. “She’s already worried about the burglary at Suzy’s house, this will just make it infinitely worse.” Everyone nodded in silent agreement. “But … poor Anastasia.” Everyone nodded again, more vigorously this time.

“She’s okay,” Bethany said. “She’s sad about the loss of the pocket watch because it was her grandfather’s and they had a special bond, but nothing else was stolen or harmed, so she’s grateful for that.”

“I’m glad to hear that,” Elnora said earnestly. “And I really hope this nightmare is over. I miss our quiet little town.”

“Agreed,” Bethany said, and the others nodded again.

No sooner had the dismissal bell rang than Elnora was out the classroom door with her bag. She had chosen to drive her car to work that day, something that very rarely happened, and usually only happened when she was running late, but today she was particularly grateful that her car was right there. She was home within a couple of minutes, and out the front door of her house in her walking clothes and shoes shortly thereafter. The pace she set as she moved down Cedar Street was far faster than her normal pace, and by the time she reached Main Street she was breathing a little more heavily than usual, but it felt good and she picked up the pace even more as she stepped onto the beach.

Elnora was normally incredibly grateful for those rare days when all of her students were engaged and interested in learning. Today, however, Elnora would have welcomed one of their more rambunctious days, simply because it would've helped to distract her from her thoughts. Regardless of the fact that both of the burglaries had been mild, with no property damage, fairly minor property loss, and no physical injuries or harm, it was still disquieting to consider that someone in their small town was robbing others. It entirely changed how Elnora felt about the sleepy little town she had grown up in and lived in her entire life--it was tainted somehow. The worst part was that she couldn't make sense of it--the burglaries were so small that they were all the more personal and offensive. It reminded her of when she caught a peeping Tom during her college years--the kid had been rude but harmless, and yet she had felt uncomfortable in her own room for many months after the incident.

Considering the burglar's apparently eclectic tastes, Elnora felt fairly certain that she didn't possess anything--openly displayed or carefully hidden away--that was in danger of being taken. Unfortunately, this didn't make her feel much better. It was like expecting an earthquake at any moment--instead of the knowledge serving to calm her down, it only made her more nervous. She hadn't been lying when she told Stan, Bethany and the others that she hoped it was over, but deep down she had a feeling that it was only just beginning.

"Wow, you look like you're on a mission," the voice came from in front of her, and Elnora raised her eyes from the sand at her feet to meet Kevin's smiling face. He had somehow been ahead of her, a strange idea considering how quickly she had gotten from the school to her house and then to the beach--perhaps he had gone straight from the school to the beach and had been jogging? He was on his way back toward town, but he turned to join her as she continued her walk north. "Hard day in the classroom?" he said, and Elnora slowed her pace.

"Actually, it was a good day in the classroom," Elnora admitted honestly. "The students were surprisingly mild-mannered and super engaged for a Monday."

"So what's bothering you?" Kevin persisted, and Elnora looked over at him. "It's pretty obvious that *something* is bothering you--you're practically sprinting." Elnora realized he was right, and slowed her pace even further.

"I'm just thinking," Elnora explained, remembering Kevin's odd behavior on the trail yesterday.

"That's some deep thinking," Kevin said, looking over at Elnora again. Something about his voice and manner made her relax, and she shrugged.

"It's complicated," she offered, looking back down at the sand and sighing.

"Well we have a lot of beach and plenty of time," Kevin gestured around them. Elnora sighed again.

"Have you heard … there's been … some lost items in town over the last week or so," Elnora said vaguely.

"Lost?" Kevin asked. "Lost how?"

"Like … taken," Elnora explained.

"Taken? You mean stolen?"

"Well … yes," Elnora admitted.

"So there's been a couple of burglaries in the last week or so?" Kevin clarified.

"Yes," Elnora said.

"Big ones?" Kevin asked.

"No," Elnora answered.

"This is like twenty questions," Kevin said. "Are you going to make me dig for the whole story?" Elnora smiled sheepishly.

"I'm sorry," Elnora apologized. "I'm just a little distracted."

"That I realized," Kevin said. "So … would you like to tell me what happened?"

"Okay," Elnora said, still hesitating. Despite the fact that gossip was the primary way she learned about everything that was happening in Blue Whale Cove, she herself wasn't much of a gossip. She felt that there was always a chance she was passing along tidbits that weren't factual, either because she had heard them wrong or remembered them wrong. It was much like the game of "telephone" her students liked to play--whatever word or sentence went in at the beginning of the line, it was sure to be changed by the time it reached the end of the line.

Elnora decided to stick to the bare minimum--the points that she felt certain of--and described for Kevin how Suzy had discovered the missing egg pendant and how she heard that Anastasia had discovered the missing pocket watch. It took her all of two minutes, with Kevin listening carefully the whole time. When she finished telling him what she knew, she shrugged her shoulders. Kevin cleared his throat.

"Well I'm not going to tell you that it's nothing, because it's definitely not nothing," Kevin said, skirting a particularly persistent wave that kept creeping toward him. "But I do think it's important to recognize that this is on the lighter side, as far as home burglaries go. I mean, no one was hurt--that's a big one--it seems that only one thing was taken from each place?" Kevin looked to Elnora for confirmation. Elnora paused, and then decided against telling Kevin about the other items Suzy had discovered were missing, and nodded. "And there was very little, if any, property damage. I think it's okay to feel a little grateful for that," Kevin said.

"I know, and I do. It's just that ..." Elnora paused, searching for the right words, "This is the sort of thing you read about happening in other places. It's not the sort of thing that happens in Blue Whale Cove. Does that make sense?" she glanced over at Kevin, who had a thoughtful look on his face.

"It makes sense that you love your town, and you've become comfortable with the fact that it's secure and safe. These burglaries alter your view of and feeling about your town and I understand why that's upsetting."

"That *is* the part that has me feeling the most disconcerted," Elnora admitted. "Of course, I feel bad for Suzy and Anastasia and I'm glad they're not hurt and not much was taken or damaged. But the thing that really bothers me is the fact that the image I've had of this town is somewhat shattered. It's like finding out that your best friend is really a spy--you begin to question if anything you experienced was real, or if it was all just part of the lie. Like what if this town has never been as secure and safe as I thought it was; I just never heard about the things that were happening?" Elnora stopped walking. She had reached her normal turning point, but she wasn't sure whether she was ready to head back to town. She felt like she had enough energy to walk forever, and if she turned back now, she was worried she would arrive back home with the feeling that she wasn't done. Kevin stopped too, and turned toward her.

"That's a pretty tricky way to go," Kevin said, looking at Elnora. She furrowed her brow, and he continued, "The 'what if' game, I mean. You could 'what if' for an eternity without solving the problem, making yourself all the more upset and worried at the same time." Elnora nodded, conceding his point. "The unfortunate fact is that there's really nothing you can do about it," Kevin said it casually and honestly, but it still made Elnora feel bad. "So what's the point in worrying about it?"

"There *is* no point in worrying about it," Elnora acknowledged. "That doesn't mean I won't worry about it. Or that no one else will worry about it," Elnora sounded like a petulant child, which she hadn't meant to do, but when she looked at Kevin he seemed unoffended. She turned her body back toward town, but didn't move to walk in that direction. Kevin turned slightly, matching her movements.

"Look, I didn't mean you should be heartless and uncaring about it," Kevin clarified.

"I know," Elnora said, meeting his eyes. "You're just trying to give me the same advice I always give others," she smiled lightly.

"Well great minds do think alike," Kevin offered, and Elnora laughed. Kevin smiled. "How about we talk about something else?" Kevin asked, and Elnora nodded gratefully.

"Yes please," Elnora said, and she began to walk again, even more slowly this time. Kevin fell into stride beside her, and the conversation naturally turned to work, their challenges and triumphs and why they loved it all. Once again, Elnora felt like there were no facades, just honest sincerity, and any doubts she had experienced about Kevin fell away.

As they approached Main Street, Elnora slowed and turned toward Kevin.

"Would you like to come over for some tea?" the words were out of her mouth before she realized she had even thought them, and she felt a blush rise to her cheeks. Kevin made a pained face.

"I would love to," Kevin said. Elnora sucked in and held her breath, waiting for the "but" that she was certain was coming. She felt disappointed, and she tried not to show it on her face. "I'm afraid that I'm rather behind in my planning," Kevin continued, sounding embarrassed. "I meant to get the week fully planned out this past weekend, but I ended up doing other things first and I ran out of time. My last lesson of today was one of those 'spur of the moment', 'fly by the seat of your pants' deals. I really should get that handled and wrap up my planning for the week so it doesn't happen again. But," Kevin added in a hopeful voice, "Perhaps a walk and tea with you tomorrow could be my reward for working hard tonight?" Elnora smiled at the hopeful, child-like quality in his voice.

"I'd love that," Elnora blushed again at the eagerness she heard in her own voice. Kevin smiled and turned north on Main Street.

"Until tomorrow then?" he asked over his shoulder.

"Until tomorrow," Elnora repeated, watching his back for a few more steps before heading up Cedar Street toward home, a deep smile affixed to her face.

CHAPTER 19

Elnora watched her students file out the classroom door and into the hallway, and she immediately headed down to the lounge. She felt excited, like she was waiting for something, and she soon realized that she was hoping to run into Kevin, even though he rarely set foot in the lounge. As she pushed open the door, her heart pitter-pattering in her chest, she scanned the room and realized he wasn't there. The crushing disappointment she immediately felt surprised her, especially since it felt like the reaction of a teenager, rather than a mature woman.

Growing up, Elnora had not experienced the typical dating scene that her peers all worked their way through. She had gone out on a couple of dates during her time in high school and college, but she hadn't really been in any relationships--certainly nothing serious or steady. And while she had experienced the normal butterflies of excitement before and during her dates, she didn't remember feeling like she couldn't wait to see the guy again, or like she wanted to spend all her time with him. She barely knew Kevin, but the little voice in the back of her mind seemed insistent on pointing out that he was special. While she relished the feeling, she also consciously put up her guard. She wasn't ready to openly admit to anyone that she may like Kevin, mostly because she wasn't entirely ready to admit it to herself.

Elnora prepared herself a cup of tea and then walked over to sit with Stan and Chrissy. They were discussing the merits of several of the books that were new on the reading program, and while this was something Elnora would normally gladly join in on, today she was content to sit quietly on the periphery of the conversation. She looked up at the clock and willed it to move more quickly. *Just five more hours …*

Elnora stepped onto the beach and paused, looking around. She was worried that she was late and Kevin was already ahead of her, though she assumed he would've waited since they had made plans to walk together. She had spent far longer getting ready than she normally did, something she had felt was foolish even as she did it. She had tried tying her hair back in a ponytail, but was dissatisfied with the way it looked and so had left it down. She had brushed her teeth and dusted her face lightly with a finishing powder before finishing up with a slightly tinted lip gloss she found in her bathroom drawer and couldn't remember when it had been purchased. When she looked at herself in the mirror, she was embarrassed to discover that her efforts were painfully obvious, and she wiped her face and lips with tissues to remove the excess powder and lip gloss. The final effect of all this was a subtle, natural flush that she decided was exactly what she wanted, even if it hadn't been achieved deliberately.

Elnora contented herself with the idea that Kevin wasn't on the beach yet, and turned toward the ocean. It was a beautiful afternoon, with clear, blue skies and a warm sun. Elnora closed her eyes, enjoying the warmth of the sun on her face and listening to the gently rolling waves. A hand fell softly onto her shoulder and she smiled, but then started at the sound of the voice, her eyes flying open.

"I'm reluctant to disturb you," Chrissy said, smiling at the look of surprise on Elnora's face. "But I can see why you like coming out here every day," Chrissy waved toward the ocean. "It's beautiful."

Elnora glanced at Chrissy, and then all around her, before realizing that Chrissy was watching her expectantly. "You startled me," Elnora smiled at her friend.

Chrissy nodded. "I can see that. I'm sorry, I didn't mean to," Chrissy's face was a mask of apology, and Elnora patted her gently on the back.

"I know. I was just enjoying the weather for a moment, before starting my walk," Elnora said, her eyes still searching the beach around them.

"I can definitely understand that," Chrissy said, turning toward the ocean and closing her eyes. "The sun is so nice and warm today, I decided to stay outside a little longer. Then I thought, why not try this fantastic walk you're always talking about? I hope you don't mind," Chrissy added, noticing the look of preoccupation in Elnora's eyes.

"Of course I don't mind," Elnora said sincerely, her eyes widening and her heart speeding up a bit as she recognized the shape coming over the small sand dunes and onto the beach toward them. Chrissy turned to follow her friend's eyes, and a look of recognition crossed her face.

"Oh no," Chrissy said quietly. "I'm so sorry, I didn't know ..."

"It's okay," Elnora said earnestly, placing her hand on Chrissy's arm. Chrissy looked at her friend's smiling face. "We can all walk together."

"Hello ladies," Kevin said easily as he approached them. They both nodded and smiled in acknowledgement. "Sorry I'm late," he looked directly at Elnora as he said this, "I took a call from my mom," he shrugged, knowing that no further explanation was necessary. All three of them had good relationships with their mothers, but they knew that "mom calls" could last anywhere from five minutes to two hours. Kevin turned toward Chrissy and smiled. "It's nice that you can join us, Chrissy. Especially on such a beautiful day," Kevin's voice was polite, but Elnora thought she also detected a slight hint of disappointment. Whether the disappointment was real or not, it didn't show on his face, and Chrissy was dutifully flattered.

"Elnora's always telling me how nice her daily walks are and encouraging me to try them, so I thought I would," Chrissy said by way of explanation.

"That's very smart," Kevin said, "Of both of you." He smiled at both of them, though he lingered a fraction of a section longer when he looked at Elnora. Chrissy turned to look at her as well, and Elnora turned away, toward the north.

"Shall we?" Elnora said, starting forward. Chrissy and Kevin fell into stride beside her, matching her pace.

The first few minutes of the walk were quiet, each of them simply enjoying the pleasant weather and lovely view. Then Chrissy mentioned something about the tide and a conversation naturally evolved, winding its way through various topics until it landed on something they all had a lot to say about: the Pacific garbage patch. This topic so thoroughly absorbed them that they had walked all the way to Elnora's turning point and all the way back to town without hardly noticing it. As they stepped off the sand and onto the sidewalk running along Main Street, they all fell quiet again, aware of their imminent separation and reluctant to launch into a new topic. Chrissy stepped over to the curb and kicked first one shoe heel, then the other, against the concrete, dislodging some of the sand that had collected on her shoes. Kevin and Elnora looked at each other, Elnora's face a question and Kevin's face a gentle, smiling answer.

"Thank you both," Kevin said, "For the lovely, stimulating company. We should do this again sometime," Kevin nodded and then looked directly at Elnora, "Soon," he finished pointedly. She nodded subtly.

"I agree," Elnora said, and Chrissy nodded. Kevin made a small, waving motion with his right hand and then turned and headed up Main Street, toward the inn. Chrissy and Elnora watched him go, and then Chrissy turned toward her friend.

"He definitely likes you," Chrissy said and Elnora shrugged, though she was unable to hide the smile curling her lips. "And," Chrissy added, elbowing Elnora gently, "You really like him." Elnora turned toward her friend, surprise clearly written across her face. "Even if you don't know it, and I suspect you *do* know it," Chrissy said, "It's pretty obvious." Elnora opened her mouth to protest, but Chrissy cut her off. "If you think I mind, you're wrong," Chrissy said, and Elnora could tell that she was telling the truth. "I mean, I won't deny that he's pretty good looking and he's very nice," Chrissy shrugged. "But he's not really my type. Too nice," Chrissy said, and Elnora scoffed. "He's perfect for you," Chrissy said earnestly, and to her credit, Elnora said nothing. "But," Chrissy said pointedly and Elnora braced herself, "We still don't know much about him. And it *is* weird that he's claiming to have visited Samantha so many times though we'd never met or heard of him before." Chrissy looked over at her friend and patted her gently on the shoulder. "Just be careful, okay?" Chrissy asked. Elnora nodded.

"I will," Elnora said softly, watching Kevin's back as he moved up the street. "I promise."

"I won't come out tomorrow," Chrissy added, and Elnora turned back to face her.

"Why not? I thought you liked the walk," Elnora asked.

"I did, a lot. But I don't want to be a third wheel," Chrissy explained, motioning toward Kevin's retreating back. Elnora shook her head and opened her mouth, but Chrissy interrupted her. "It's okay. I'll still walk, I promise. Maybe I'll come out here and walk south or something. Or just through town. It'll be fine," Chrissy assured her friend. "You walked alone for years and loved it, I want to see what all the fuss is about." Elnora smiled widely at this.

"Thank you," Elnora said, and squeezed Chrissy's shoulder in a gentle, one-handed sort of hug. Chrissy smiled back at her.

Together, they crossed the road and headed home.

CHAPTER 20

It was time again, something they had no doubt about but also found disquieting.

The urges were suddenly coming more frequently and strongly, and they simultaneously brought a feeling of urgency that had never been experienced before.

That urgency was dangerous, as it could lead to rash actions--the very kind that made it difficult to remain concealed.

Nonetheless, the bigger problem now was the lack of focus or sleep caused by the itch.

A new item pervaded their thoughts.

It had to be acquired.

Soon.

CHAPTER 21

Just after 6:00 am on Tuesday, March 13th, Frances Brexton stepped into her garage, turned on the light, and made her way over to the small worker's table that sat against the eastern wall. The table held a collection of small tools that her husband used for various handiwork around the house, along with a large blue bucket of gardening tools. Frances grabbed the bucket, picked up her leather gardening gloves, stepped into her gardening boots, shut off the overhead light and opened the garage door. Her car sat alone on one side of the driveway--her husband, Harold, was a logger and had recently been shipped out to a location down south. He had left Monday morning and he would return Thursday afternoon. Frances never slept terribly well when he was gone, and she often used the early morning hours to work in her garden. It was a secret pleasure to be quietly digging in the dirt, feeling like the only living thing that was awake in the entire world, as the sun slowly rose over the horizon.

Frances walked over to the western edge of her property, set the bucket down and knelt in the dirt, tackling the weeds growing therein.

Just a few minutes later, a shadow crept out of the bushes on the eastern side of the Brexton property, stole across the driveway into the darkened garage, quietly opened the door and slipped into the house.

About two minutes later, just as the sun was beginning to flood the sky with soft light, the door from the garage into Frances' house opened, and the shadow passed through into the garage, closing the door softly behind them. For a moment the shadow was completely undetectable, as it remained entirely still, listening for the sounds of Frances' claw weeder in the dirt. The rhythmic sound of digging filtered back to the garage and the shadow finally moved, quickly, out of the garage, across the driveway, and back into the bushes at the eastern side of the property.

After spending an hour in her garden and accumulating a considerable pile of pulled weeds, Frances sat back on her heels, wiped the back of her arm against her forehead, and looked up at the beautiful blue sky. The sounds of birds awakening to the new day had grown from a dim chirping to a loud, persistent twittering, and Frances knew it was time to go inside and get ready for work. She pushed herself up onto her feet, put her gardening tools back into the blue bucket on top of the pile of weeds she had pulled, and made her way back to the garage. She pulled the gardening tools out of the bucket, dumped the contents of the bucket into the green clippings receptacle, placed the tools back in the bucket, and put the bucket onto the worker's table. Frances then stepped out of her gardening boots, closed the garage door, opened the door into her house and stepped inside.

Moments later, Frances stood in front of her master

shower, adjusting the temperature of the water. She pulled off her clothes, placing them in the laundry hamper that sat in the corner across from the double sinks, and stepped into the warm water, pulling the shower door closed behind her.

After a long, hot shower, Frances shut off the water, pushed open the shower door and stepped out onto the thick, soft bath mat. She grabbed the towel from the hook next to the shower and toweled off, wrapping her wet hair in the towel as a finishing touch. She stepped into the large walk-in closet and selected her clothing for the day--a lavender linen dress with delicate white flowers embroidered along the bottom hem.

Twenty minutes later, fully dressed, with her face made up and hair dried, Frances opened the bathroom door and stepped into her bedroom. On top of the low seven-drawer dresser sat the beautiful walnut burl jewelry box her husband had given her two years earlier, on her thirty-fifth birthday. The finishing touch for her outfit sat in the jewelry box, and she felt a rush of excitement.

Frances gently pulled open the bottom drawer and gasped when she saw the empty, black-velvet-lined space.

The antique Georgian amethyst brooch pendant, the only heirloom Frances' mother's family had ever possessed, was missing.

CHAPTER 22

Elnora stepped onto the sandy beach and breathed deeply, pulling the salty sea air deep into her lungs. Even after a long day in the classroom, Elnora felt energized and itching for her walk. She looked all around her and, seeing no one, decided to head north along the beach, slowly.

It had been exactly the sort of challenging and busy day that Elnora had needed in order to keep her mind on her work. She had known from the moment her students walked into her classroom that morning and sat down that it would be a challenging day. The energy in the room felt different--electric. Elnora became very alert and watchful, spotting and handling all sorts of oddities throughout the remainder of the day.

Elnora had discovered long ago that second graders could get into two main types of trouble. The first type was loud and blatant, like when one student complained that another had taken the toy they had been playing with and then pushed the offending student hard, right in plain view. The second type was stealthy and sneaky, like when a student sat in the puzzle corner quietly, head bent forward over the puzzle, and twenty minutes later finally revealed that they had actually been quietly working with scissors the whole time, cutting themselves some new bangs.

Neither type of trouble was desirable, of course, but the latter type was by far the worse of the two. With the first type, Elnora could turn her back to her students to write on the dry-erase board at the front of the room or change the display on one of her boards, and the students would quickly alert her whenever she needed to step in and help with a situation. With the second type, Elnora had to remain alert and vigilant, knowing full well that should one student require her attention, even for one minute, that was enough time for another student to get into something. And then she would spend the rest of the day figuring out how to explain the situation to the child's parents. That was, understandably, often the most difficult part. She had to figure out how to place full responsibility for their actions in the student's hands without appearing to accuse the student or abandon her own responsibility.

Today, she had walked out with her students to the drop-off and pick-up stations lining the front of the building in order to explain two situations to two sets of parents. Ironically, both of the situations had occurred during the last period of the day, when Elnora was typically the most tired and the least alert. She had allowed for a quiet coloring period at the end of their geography seminar. It allowed all of them a moment to sit and relax, listening to classical music and creating. Her students had been very much in agreement with this plan, and they were even quieter and more focused than usual. Of course, this alerted Elnora even more, because after the sort of day they had just experienced, her students suddenly turning 180 degrees was a bit bizarre. After scanning the room for five minutes and seeing nothing, Elnora had stood up and walked the aisles. And it was then she discovered that Polly had somehow found a black Sharpie marker and was drawing a beautiful, semi-permanent tattoo on her left hand and arm. By the time she had Polly up and over to the sink to wash off as much of the marker as she possibly could, Elnora knew she was in trouble. She scanned the room again and, noticing that Charlie's head was a bit too close to his table to be normal or comfortable, she walked over and caught Charlie creating a beautiful drawing … on his white t-shirt.

The good news was that Polly's tattoo would fade away within a day or two, and Charlie's shirt should wash right back to white with a little careful laundering, but nonetheless, Elnora knew it would be best if she explained the situation to the students' parents. This way, they would shake their heads and laugh about "that kid." If Elnora didn't explain the situation in person right away, however, the parents may not be terribly upset, but there was a chance that they would wonder, if only for a second, what was going on in "that classroom." As it happened, both Polly's father and Charlie's mother were amused and slightly embarrassed by their child's antics, and they both thanked Elnora for preventing their kids from doing anything worse. Elnora had accepted the acknowledgements, while still feeling slightly guilty that she hadn't prevented either situation entirely.

Elnora's mind came back to the present and she suddenly realized that she was walking at her normal pace, and she was halfway to her turning point. She slowed for a moment and turned, walking backwards for a few steps while scanning the beach to the south. She saw nothing and no one behind her, shrugged as if to push off the wave of disappointment that flooded her, turned back north, and continued her walk.

An hour later, Elnora returned to Main Street and stood waiting patiently for a break between cars so that she could cross the street. She took advantage of a small window created by a car that was moving exceptionally slowly and jogged lightly across the street. Impulsively, she angled to the right so she could look in through the windows of Blue Whale Cove Trinkets. The window displays had been well-arranged, with a collection of interesting items that were eye-catching but not overwhelming. There was a collection of colorful spoon rests, some rubber trivets and potholders, an adorable cupcake pan that made mini-cupcakes shaped like sea animals, hand towels in soft blues and greens, and a few other items. As Elnora continued to window shop, she saw motion at the back of the store and looked up to see Frances Brexton approaching.

Frances had also grown up in Blue Whale Cove, and though her mother was still the legal owner of Blue Whale Cove Trinkets, everyone in town recognized that Trinkets was really Frances' store now. Like her mother, Frances was petite and full-figured, with long blonde hair and ocean blue eyes. Elnora smiled as Frances stepped through the open doorway.

"Won't you come in?" Frances asked. Elnora shrugged and then nodded, following Frances into the store. "On your way back from your walk?" Frances asked as they moved toward the back of the store.

"Uh-huh," Elnora said, her eyes alighting on a beautiful set of delicate China teacups. She turned and moved closer, reaching to pick up a cup. Frances noticed and turned with her.

"Aren't they beautiful? They just came in last week," Frances said.

Elnora traced her finger softly over the rose painted on the side. "They're hand painted?" she said in surprise. Frances nodded. "They're beautiful," Elnora agreed, replacing the cup on its saucer.

"I've already sold two sets," Frances said proudly. "Both to tourists."

"They always get the good stuff," Elnora said in mock-disappointment and Frances laughed.

"So, how have you been? It's been ages since we last talked," Frances pulled a stool out from behind the sales counter and indicated to it. Elnora stepped over and took a seat as Frances pulled out a second stool and took a seat.

"Busy, but good," Elnora said.

"How many do you have this year?"

"Twenty," Elnora said.

"You have the patience of a saint," Frances said. "I love kids, really I do, but I don't know if I could handle so many of them at once," she smiled softly.

"I feel the same way about running the inventory of a small store," Elnora responded and Frances' smile deepened. "But then I think it's supposed to be that way--we each have our own strengths, and that's what allows us to do what we do. I could never be a doctor, but thank goodness there are others who can!" Frances nodded.

"Touché!"

"How about you, how have you been?" Elnora asked, and she immediately saw the shadow darken Frances' face. "What's wrong?"

Frances saw the look of deep concern on Elnora's face and forced a smile. "Oh, it's okay, I just ..." her eyes became wet and Elnora stood, alarmed at the sudden, sharp reaction she had unintentionally caused. "No, no, I'm okay. I guess it just suddenly hit me," Frances said, carefully dabbing at her eyes with a tissue.

"What just hit you? Is something wrong?" Elnora asked, her voice filled with concern.

"My amethyst brooch is missing," Frances' voice cracked as she forced the words out.

"Oh I'm so sorry! Do you have any idea where it may be?" Elnora asked, relieved that it was nothing worse, as she had initially feared it might be. It had been awhile since she had last seen Frances' mother, and it was well-known that she had been suffering poor health for awhile now, which was why Frances ran the store most of the time.

"I think it was taken," Frances said, her voice beginning to strengthen. Elnora frowned.

"Taken? You mean … stolen?" Elnora was surprised at how difficult it was to say the word. Frances nodded. "Are you sure?" Elnora asked. "Is it possible that it's just misplaced?" Frances shook her head.

"I saw it in my jewelry box last night. That's why I decided to wear my lavender dress today," she looked down, as if to verify the dress was still there. "Harold is down south on a job until Thursday, so it's just me in the house." Frances froze, and a look of fear crossed her face. "That means someone was in my house," Frances choked out, and Elnora placed a reassuring hand on her arm.

"Have you filed a police report?" Elnora asked, and Frances shook her head.

"No. I guess I'm hoping that I'll go home and find it, even though I'm positive it's not there. I already checked all the obvious places this morning as soon as I realized it was missing, and it was nowhere to be found. The weirdest part about it," Frances said, looking off over Elnora's head and thinking, "Is that nothing else seems to be missing. Just that. And it wasn't out in the open or anything, so it had to have been someone who knows me well, and knows my house. But who would do such a thing?" Frances looked back at Elnora.

"I have no idea," Elnora said, and meant it.

CHAPTER 23

BLUE WHALE COVE, OR -- Blue Whale Cove homeowners are encouraged to lock their doors and windows in response to a series of home burglaries over the past two weeks.

"We are proud of our small, safe city," Blue Whale Cove Chief of Police, Douglas Hinson, told the Blue Whale Cove Journal. "It's quiet and calm, and we don't have a lot of crime. It's understandable that three home burglaries in a little over a week has everybody a bit nervous. Residents should exercise caution, secure their homes, and remain alert."

The first burglary occurred on Sunday, March 4th, and only one item was reported as missing. The second burglary occurred on Saturday, March 10th, and the third burglary occurred on Tuesday, March 13th, and again only one item was reported missing each time. No one has been hurt during the burglaries, and it appears the burglar gained access to the homes through unlocked doors and windows.

Chief Hinson indicates that investigations are under way, but there are currently no suspects.

Residents are understandably concerned.

"We haven't had anything like this happen in Blue Whale Cove as long as I've been here," a long-term resident said, "And all of a sudden there's multiple break-ins, but no one really understands why."

"It really destroys the feeling of safety," another resident said.

"I've gotten used to just going about my business with no worries," another resident said. "Now I have to be sure to always check my doors and windows. It makes me feel like I shouldn't go out anymore."

Chief Hinson says that they plan to boost police presence in the city, with some help from the neighboring Tillamook Police Department, and he encourages residents to consider installing video doorbells. On Saturday, March 17th at 9:00 am in the Blue Whale Cove Recreation Center on 3rd Street, Chief Hinson and Mayor Nassau will hold a community gathering to update residents and provide further advice on how to stay safe.

CHAPTER 24

Elnora set down the newspaper and sank back into the cushions on her couch. She was exhausted, and due at work in an hour.

Elnora had slept fitfully the night before, experiencing a series of dreams that had no real beginning, end or meaning, but somehow made her feel nervous and like she was forgetting something important. She awoke fully at 4:00 am, and after a quick trip to the restroom she realized that there was no way she would fall back asleep. She crept into her living room and turned on the light, glancing at the book lying on the coffee table. She considered it for a moment, and then returned to her bedroom and put on her walking clothes, putting an extra layer of light clothing on underneath in order to help keep her warm in the cool morning air.

The street lights bathed the streets and sidewalks with a soft yellow glow. Normally, on the rare occasions that Elnora went out this early, the small, bright pools of light made

Elnora feel safe--like she was protected by the light. This morning, however, the light felt cool and foreign, and Elnora hurried through them toward the beach, where there would be little light at all until the sun rose in a couple of hours.

As Elnora headed north on the beach, she passed the few residential houses, Suzy Busterson's among them, that hugged the beach. She noticed that Suzy had multiple lights on in her house, and she was fairly certain it would remain that way for awhile. She was also fairly certain that Suzy had started to lock her back door when she went out for her morning jogs, though she had no way to confirm whether this was true.

Elnora passed the final house lining the beach and focused on the darkness ahead of her. There was only the subtle light thrown down by the moon and reflected back from the inky black of the ocean to help light her way. She sped up her pace, walking so quickly that she was almost jogging, and tried to push thoughts of burglary from her mind.

By the time Elnora reached her turning point she had worked up a good sweat and had managed to shift her attention. She was going to stop by Misty's house again and visit with Misty and Sophia Rose, and thoughts of the adorable baby girl were sufficient to push back other thoughts, though they still hung near the periphery of her mind.

Elnora had walked about a hundred yards south when she suddenly stopped. In the distance a dark shadow was rapidly approaching. Elnora felt a wave of panic and her heart began to pound loudly in her chest, nearly drowning out the sound of the gentle waves.

Elnora's first instinct was to get out of the way and hide, but there was absolutely nowhere for her to go--unless, of course, she turned around and headed back to the north. She considered moving further east, toward the edge of the beach and Hwy 101, or further west, toward the water, but as she watched the approaching shadow she wasn't sure that moving in either direction would make her invisible.

The shadow continued to grow in size as it approached, and Elnora imagined it was very slender but at least six feet tall. She felt paralyzed, like she couldn't move to the left or right even if she wanted to, and simply had to face what was coming.

Within fifty feet of Elnora, the outline of the shadow defined itself into precise lines, and Elnora realized it wasn't quite as tall as she had first suspected. She relaxed slightly, letting out the breath she hadn't realized she was holding.

As the shadow closed the final twenty feet of distance between them, Elnora felt enormous relief and waved a hand at Suzy Busterson as she jogged past her. Suzy nodded in acknowledgement and continued past Elnora, her breathing rhythmic and regular.

Elnora felt the flood of exhaustion that follows a sudden rise and then drop of adrenaline, and pushed herself to start walking south again. By the time she came off the beach to cross Main Street, Elnora felt exhausted. She knew she needed to get some breakfast into her.

It was the newsstand on the corner of Main Street and Cedar Street that caught Elnora's attention. She saw the story on the front page and started to read it through the plastic door. She got halfway down the story when another resident, someone she recognized but couldn't recall the name of, stepped up beside her to buy a paper. She apologized and moved out of the way while he pushed coins into the machine and pulled open the door. He pulled out his paper and then held the door open, indicating with his head for her to grab one. She pulled one out, telling herself she would stop by later to put the coins in, and he winked at her as he let the door close.

Elnora carried the paper home and finished reading the short article while sitting on her couch. Eventually, she forced herself to get up and fix some scrambled eggs, though she barely ate two bites of them. She stood for an eternity under the hot water in the shower, her mind completely preoccupied. Somehow she got out and got dressed, dried and brushed her hair, and got out to her car on time.

Elnora placed the key in her car door and opened the lock and door, and then stood there for a moment. The town was quiet, like it always was, but she swore she could feel the difference in the town around her. It felt changed somehow, like it had lost its innocence.

CHAPTER 25

Between her physical exhaustion and mental preoccupation, Elnora operated all day through a thin veil that hid the details of everything around her. As they were wont to do, her students recognized that something was awry with their teacher and decided to take full advantage--trying things they normally never tried because they knew that they couldn't get away with them. Halfway through handwriting, Elnora suddenly realized that nearly every student was using pens or markers, rather than pencils. When she asked them to get the proper writing utensils, the students groaned with disappointment, but it sounded different to her. It was not the disappointment of being asked to stop something they had wanted to do, but rather the disappointment of being interrupted in the middle of a game. Elnora's long experience as a 2nd grade teacher warned her that she had better become more alert, or it was bound to be a day full of "testing" games. Her resolve and focus lasted a whole five minutes.

By the end of the day, Elnora had uncovered three glitter glue "decorations" on student desks, five pencils that had been sharpened on both ends, another four pencils that had been sharpened down to two-inch sticks, three erasers that were utterly useless as they had large pieces of pencil lead poking out of every side, and five spelling homework papers that had been used as drawing pages. Elnora sighed as she cleaned up the messes and discarded the newly-created waste. She knew better than to let herself remain distracted through a single period, let alone an entire school day, but she just hadn't been able to help it. She hoped that an afternoon spent cuddling an adorable baby would have better luck at distracting her from her thoughts and bringing her back to reality.

"Well hello, little girl," Elnora cooed at the baby girl staring up at her with big, brown eyes. "How are you today?" Sophia continued to stare curiously at Elnora, and then she suddenly revealed a big, gummy grin. "What a beautiful smile," Elnora acknowledged, "Thank you!" Sophia grinned again, and gently kicked her legs. "Oh, so strong!" she laughed softly, watching the baby show off.

"So, what's the news?" Misty asked, watching her daughter and her friend.

Elnora kept her eyes on Sophia, but turned her head slightly toward Misty. "What news?"

"What news? Isn't the whole town buzzing with news about the burglaries?" Misty asked. "I don't get out and Justin works in Tillamook--you're my only line to the real world!"

Elnora looked at her friend and smiled. "You haven't been out yet?"

Misty shook her head. "I have everything I need here, and she's so tiny in that huge carseat, it just feels weird. But even though I love spending time with her," Sophia cooed and Misty paused, a huge smile taking over her face, "I'm definitely getting cabin fever."

Elnora nodded. "I completely understand. Maybe you could wrap her up in that … what is that wrap thing you have?" Elnora paused and looked at Misty.

"The Moby wrap?" Misty offered.

Elnora nodded again. "Yeah, that. You could wrap her up so she's cuddled up right with you, and then go for a walk. The weather has been really nice lately--unseasonably warm."

"Yeah, maybe. But in the meantime, you have to be my gossip-bringer," Misty said expectantly.

Elnora paused, looking back down at Sophia's face. "I don't know that I have much to share," Elnora shrugged. It was true that she had some details of each burglary, but they were details that she felt certain were common knowledge by now. She was full of questions, confusions and speculations, but she would rather not share those.

"That can't be true," Misty argued.

"Well what *do* you know?" Elnora asked, smiling back down at Sophia. Sophia opened her mouth wide in a huge yawn and blinked her eyes.

"I know that Suzy is missing her egg pendant, Anastasia is missing her enamel pocket watch and Frances is missing her amethyst brooch," Misty ticked each item off on her fingers.

Elnora nodded, her eyes on Sophia's increasingly droopy ones. "I honestly don't know much more than that," Elnora softly replied. "I know that nothing else seems to have been taken in each case, and that the burglar apparently got in through unlocked windows and doors, and that's all."

Elnora thought about the trouble Suzy was having with her insurance company, and the additional missing items, but decided to say nothing about this.

"It's so strange," Misty whispered, glancing down at Sophia as the baby finally closed her eyes fully. "I mean, who would go through all the trouble, and the risk, to break into someone's house--just to take a single item? A single item that they likely can't sell, no less," Misty shrugged. Elnora remained quiet; these were the same questions that had been running through her head, and she was no closer to solving them than when they had first arisen. "But I think the creepiest part is the fact that the burglar *must* be from Blue Whale Cove," Misty shivered involuntarily. "True, Suzy's egg pendant was openly on display in her hallway, but that wasn't the case for Anastasia's pocket watch or Frances' brooch." Misty paused, looking at Elnora. "I keep wondering who knew all three of them well enough to know about those items, and the trouble is that the answer is *everyone.* Literally everyone in town must have known in one way or another, don't you think? I mean, we've all seen the egg pendant at Suzy's holiday parties, and I remember that when I was younger Anastasia loved to tell stories of her grandfather and show everyone his pocket watch. Frances' brooch is gorgeous, and though she only wears it once a month or so, everyone notices it."

Elnora nodded, admiring the fact that Misty's train of thought on the subject closely followed her own. "True."

"But then, if it *is* someone in town, what on Earth do they expect to do with these things? They can't display them. Or wear them. Or sell them!" Misty finished.

Elnora shrugged, "I don't know. It really is a mystery."

"Well I know it seems a little silly, but I've asked Justin to install a security system," Misty said. "Surprisingly, he didn't argue at all!" Misty's whispered tones betrayed her surprise. Elnora smiled. Misty's husband loved to tease her about being an excessive worry-wort. However, he was surely mindful of the fact that Misty was alone at home with their newborn daughter while there was a burglar on the loose--and he worked too far away to be of help should an emergency arise. It was possible he had already been considering installing a security system, and was relieved when his wife--the worry-wort--mentioned it first.

"That's a good idea," Elnora agreed.

Misty nodded, obviously relieved that Elnora agreed with her. "I just hope this is over soon," she added.

"Me too," Elnora said, looking into her friend's eyes, and then back down at the sleeping baby in her arms.

Elnora stayed for another hour and the conversation turned to happier topics, like how much weight Misty had already lost post-delivery. Elnora finally excused herself at 5:30 pm, when her stomach was firmly telling her it was time to eat dinner. She handed Sophia back to her mother, promised to visit again soon, and made her way back home.

As Elnora opened the door into her house, she stopped short. The light in the kitchen was on. She never left the lights on when she left the house, and though she had been undeniably exhausted and preoccupied when she had left earlier, she was nonetheless certain that she hadn't left any lights on.

Elnora had unlocked the front door when she came home just now, of that she was positive. She worked her way around the entire house, checking the door into the garage and the door into the backyard, as well as all of the windows. Everything was firmly shut and locked, and from what she could tell, absolutely nothing was out of place or missing.

Finally, thirty minutes after she had stepped through her

front door, Elnora decided that no one could have been in her home, and that this was just the first time she had left her kitchen light on when leaving the house. She quickly fixed herself a turkey and cheese sandwich and sat on the couch to watch a movie, hoping that this would serve to empty her mind at last. Halfway through her movie, she realized she was nodding off and should head to bed, but instead she pulled the soft throw blanket off the back of the couch, turned the volume down on the movie, and lay down on her side, closing her eyes and drifting off to sleep.

CHAPTER 26

Elnora awoke on Thursday morning, feeling incredibly well-rested and refreshed despite having slept all night on her couch. Fortunately, her television had shut itself off after the movie had finished, leaving her in the quiet darkness. Despite how pleasant the experience had been, she knew better than to assume that she should make sleeping on the couch a regular thing. It was one of those flukes--when you were so exhausted that changing your sleeping location might actually work to your advantage. It reminded Elnora of when she was ill as a child; for some reason it was so much more relaxing and restful to sleep on the couch than her bed, but only for a couple of nights in a row maximum.

Elnora's students seemed to sense that their teacher was fully rested and alert, and they were on their absolute best behavior throughout their first period. As soon as they left for recess, Elnora walked down the hall to the teacher's lounge, feeling like it had been ages since she had last been in there.

Chrissy smiled up at her from their sitting area, and Elnora smiled back at her friend, stepping over to the kitchen area to prepare her cup of tea. A few moments later she took a seat across from Chrissy, cradling the warm mug in her hands.

"It's a good day, huh?" Chrissy asked, reading the cues on Elnora's face.

Elnora nodded. "Yes, thank goodness. I was so exhausted yesterday, but I slept really well last night," Elnora took a small sip of tea, relishing the feeling as the hot liquid slid down her throat. "How about you?"

Chrissy nodded. "Pretty good. This week has not been without its own challenges, but it's definitely better than last week."

"I'm happy to hear it," Elnora said, sipping her tea again.

"Where were you yesterday afternoon?" Chrissy asked, her brow furrowed. "I stopped by to visit because I saw your kitchen light on, but you didn't answer."

"I was over at Misty's again," Elnora explained. Chrissy's frown deepened.

"With your kitchen light on?"

"I know, I left it on."

"That's pretty unlike you," Chrissy said.

"I told you I was exhausted!" Elnora said in mock hurt.

"Still, that's pretty weird," Chrissy pressed, smiling at the look on her friend's face. Elnora broke her frown and smiled. "So … going for a walk tonight?" Chrissy raised her eyebrows and then winked at her friend.

"Well yes, I am," Elnora said. "Just like I do almost every single day," she emphasized each of the last three words.

"No, no," Chrissy said. "I mean … are you going for a walk with company tonight?"

"I don't know," Elnora said. "He didn't show up Tuesday night, and I haven't seen or spoken with him since."

"That's weird," Chrissy said again, more seriously this time.

Elnora shrugged. "He probably just got tied up with something important. It's really okay," Elnora told her friend, even as the voice in the back of her mind insisted, *No, it's not.*

"What's more important than keeping a date with you?" Chrissy asked.

"It wasn't a date," Elnora argued.

"Yes, it was," Chrissy retorted, though her voice was soft.

Elnora smiled at her friend, refusing to be drawn into an argument. "Why are you pushing, anyway? I thought you were suspicious of him," Elnora asked quietly. Stan was standing by the espresso machine, sipping his coffee while reading his book, but he could still hear them if they were loud enough.

"I'm not suspicious of him," Chrissy said. "I just want you to be careful. But he seems nice," Chrissy shrugged, "And he obviously likes you and you like him." She shrugged again, as though no further explanation was needed.

"I'll keep all that in mind," Elnora said, with just enough condescension to get a rise out of her friend. Chrissy gasped in mock offense, right on cue, and they both laughed.

"Wow," Chrissy sighed. "Can you believe that Spring Break is only a week away?"

"Hardly," Elnora admitted. "It's crept up on me so fast that I haven't made any plans. You?"

Chrissy shook her head. "Same. I'll probably just clean and organize the house."

"That actually sounds good," Elnora said, taking another sip of her tea. "Maybe I'll do the same. But it might be nice to get away a little bit--how about a short trip up to Seattle?"

Chrissy shrugged. "Sure, that would be nice."

The two friends finished the last of their tea in silence.

"Alright," Chrissy said finally, pushing herself up out of the chair. "Back to the grindstone?"

Elnora nodded and stood. "Back to the grindstone," she repeated. She placed her empty tea mug in the sink and they walked together out the door and down the hallway to their classrooms.

CHAPTER 27

Elnora saw him long before she reached Main Street, and felt the butterflies in her stomach a moment later. She tried hard to maintain a steady pace as she closed the distance between them, but she was certain she had sped up considerably by the time she finally reached him.

"Hello," Elnora said casually.

"Hello," Kevin responded with a smile. "I thought it would be far better to apologize in person, when I could simultaneously make up for it," he paused, as if to read her reaction before continuing. Elnora smiled and he continued, "I'm very sorry that I missed our walk together on Tuesday night. I don't really have a good excuse at all, I simply left the school with a bunch of 'homework,' got back to the inn, and completely forgot about everything else," Kevin's voice sounded pained, and Elnora's heart leapt in response. "I only realized at 8:00 pm, long after you were done walking and back home," Kevin explained. "I considered stopping by your place to offer my apologies, but I don't know where you live and I don't have any other way to contact you," Kevin continued, and Elnora was certain he sounded as heartbroken as she had felt that night when he didn't show up. "Anyway, I'm very sorry, and I hope you'll let me join you this evening."

"I appreciate your apology," Elnora said, "But it's really not necessary." *Yes, it is,* the voice in her head insisted. "I understand how things can go, especially when you're trying to get grooved in to a new class in a new location." *No, you don't,* the voice in her head argued.

"Well I feel it is necessary, so thank you for accepting it," Kevin said. Then he turned and waved an arm toward the beach. "Shall we?" Elnora nodded and they stepped together to the curb of Main Street, waiting for traffic to clear before crossing the road.

They walked for awhile in silence, enjoying the blue skies, the warm sun and the sound of the waves, before Kevin turned toward Elnora.

"How are you doing?" Kevin asked, and when Elnora turned to look at him she was surprised to find concern on his face.

"I'm well, why?" Elnora asked.

Kevin shrugged. "I guess I assumed that with another burglary in town, you might be feeling a little anxious again."

Elnora sighed, so softly that the sound was lost below the sound of the waves. "It's definitely disquieting," Elnora admitted, looking down at the sand at her feet, "And I cannot deny that it's absorbed my thoughts more and for longer than I'd like to admit," she smiled sheepishly at him, "But I don't honestly know what to think about it."

"I can't blame you," Kevin said. "It's definitely a weird one. On the one hand, someone is stealing from others. On the other hand, they're not hurting anyone, they're not destroying property, and they can't really sell the items to make money. It's not exactly logical."

"Exactly," Elnora agreed. For some reason that she couldn't understand, she felt markedly better just talking about the burglaries with Kevin. It wasn't anything more than what she had done with Misty or Chrissy, in fact it seemed like she had talked to Kevin far less overall, but he had a very matter-of-fact, unemotional way of looking at the situation that calmed her down and made her feel less anxious. "It really bothers me that all signs point to it being someone local. You know, a Blue Whale Cove resident. I may not know everyone in this town perfectly well, but I used to think I knew the residents well enough to assume that something like this couldn't happen."

"That's understandable," Kevin said.

"And then there's this strange feeling of guilt," Elnora said, surprised she was admitting that much to him, when she hadn't even admitted it to Misty or Chrissy.

"Guilt?" Kevin repeated.

"Yeah," Elnora said. She felt his eyes on her, but paused anyway, searching for the right words to describe what she was feeling. "I can't help the feeling that this individual isn't some random troublemaker, trying to stir up the town or anything like that. They're taking things that would be difficult to sell, given that the purchasers would likely want proof of provenance, and that, even if they did sell them, would be unlikely to turn a great profit--except, of course, the egg pendant, but then that would be even trickier to sell since it's registered and insured." Elnora paused and realized she was rambling a bit. To his credit, Kevin didn't seem concerned, only interested. "I can't help thinking," Elnora paused again, choosing her words carefully, "That it's someone who is mentally unstable. And," Elnora took a deep breath, "If that's true, and they're a resident of this town, I feel guilty that I haven't helped. I know that sounds ridiculous, but it's just the way I feel."

Kevin stopped and turned toward her, prompting Elnora to stop too. "It doesn't sound ridiculous," Kevin said sincerely, looking Elnora straight in the eyes. "You sound like someone who cares a lot about others. You sound like someone who feels bad when you consider that someone out there might need your help and you don't know about it." Elnora nodded absently, agreeing without meaning to. "But you have to remember that not everyone who is struggling with challenges or difficulties in their life makes them obvious to others. In fact, many individuals who are struggling with challenges or difficulties manage to hide their struggles thoroughly from even those who are closest to them. I'm sure you've heard stories about parents who are utterly shocked when they discover that their beloved, well-cared-for and well-educated child is not just doing drugs, but is hopelessly addicted to the most dangerous opiates." Elnora nodded. She had heard stories like that, and had always wondered how it was possible. "You have to remember that the individual himself must want to receive help before they will actually be able to," Kevin started to laugh and Elnora stared at him in confusion. "I'm so sorry, but I suddenly sound like I'm lecturing you, and I didn't mean to," he explained.

Elnora shrugged. "I don't feel lectured to. Please, continue," she encouraged.

Kevin smiled again. "Well I'm afraid I don't have much more advice to offer," he said, suddenly appearing shy and embarrassed. "Except perhaps one little thing--you're right that this individual may not be a troublemaker. But maybe they're not mentally ill either," Kevin paused and looked out at the ocean before looking back at Elnora, a twinkle in his eye. "Maybe they're just someone who likes pretty things."

CHAPTER 28

There was no formal invitation or acceptance, Kevin simply walked with Elnora all the way back to her house. When they arrived, she invited him in for a cup of tea and he accepted without hesitation. Elnora's heart began to beat wildly again, and the butterflies in her stomach made her feel a little light-headed, but she kept her cool (or at least thought she did) and brought him into her home.

They sat first in the kitchen and then on the couch in the living room and talked for hours. Elnora's eyes began to feel droopy and she felt incredibly tired, but she refused to look at the clock or do anything that could put an end to what seemed almost like a small moment of magic. The conversation flowed easily, and while she and Kevin had unique points of view, they also had a lot in common, and it was stimulating and validating all at once. For the first time in her life, Elnora revealed that she had read "The Great Gatsby" and didn't care for it. She went on for several minutes, explaining why she didn't like it--how it felt morose from start to finish, but in a way that she didn't really understand or empathize with. That wasn't to say, she explained, that it couldn't be an incredible read for others, and she could certainly admit that Fitzgerald had a style of writing that she really admired, but it just didn't speak to her. She went on to explain that she understood the importance of painting reality, not just sunshine and rainbows, and that the story was certainly raw and real, but again it violated the very principle behind why she liked reading fiction--to experience the sunshine, rainbows and vindication that often didn't occur in real life--and the overall tone was so depressing that she simply couldn't palate it. When she finished explaining her position, Elnora waited with bated breath, prepared for the onslaught of countering remarks she often received when she expressed an opinion that ran counter to popular opinion. To her surprise, Kevin didn't counter her at all. He had actually experienced the same difficulty when reading the book, and hadn't ever told anyone before because everyone always raved about how incredible it was. They spent a moment smiling at one another over this shared "secret," and then the conversation picked up and continued, unrolling naturally as the minutes ticked by.

Finally, when Elnora was becoming more and more alarmed by the thought that she would suddenly keel over on the couch in a deep sleep, Kevin politely excused himself and explained that it was time he went back to the inn so they could both get some sleep. Elnora stood slowly, pausing as she tried to orient herself through a mild case of exhaustion-driven dizziness, and walked him to the door.

Kevin stood in the doorway for a moment, and then suddenly leaned forward and lightly kissed Elnora's cheek before turning and walking down the driveway and out to the street. Elnora stood frozen for several moments, watching his outline fade into the light evening fog until he was only a shadow, and then he was gone.

CHAPTER 29

The itch was back.

This time, along with the usual rush of adrenaline and anticipation, it brought fear.

Fear of being caught.

Fear of being exposed.

Fear of their darkest secret being revealed.

But the itch couldn't be ignored.

The desire for something new was powerful.

Too powerful.

They could feel the overwhelming desire block out all other, rational thoughts.

The very rational thoughts that normally prevented capture.

But the itch had to be scratched.

Soon.

CHAPTER 30

Just after 12:20 pm on Friday, March 16th, Michelle Holland stepped out the front door of her house, a small pink envelope in her hand. Inside the envelope was Michelle's weekly letter to her daughter, who lived all the way across the country in New York, where she was attending the Fashion Institute of Design and Merchandising. Regardless of whether her daughter responded to her or not, and she often did, Michelle wrote and sent her a new letter every Friday. She closed the door behind her but she didn't bother to lock it, as she was only walking two blocks to the post office and would come directly back home again. At the very most, she would be gone for twenty minutes. Her roast needed to cook for another thirty minutes, and she was certainly not going to let it dry out by leaving it in the oven for longer than that.

A few moments after walking out her front door, Michelle reached the end of her block and turned the corner, disappearing from view. Immediately, a shadow that had been crouching behind the large, dense azalea bush in Michelle's front yard moved quickly to the front porch and in through her front door.

Two minutes later, Michelle's front door opened, revealing for just a moment a shadow that pulled the door shut and then disappeared behind the bushes in Michelle's front yard. Across the street, sitting in her soft, pink velvet armchair in front of her living room window and knitting a hat for her grandson, Janice Terrin thought she saw a dark shape move across the yard in front of her. She placed her knitting in her lap and picked up her glasses on the table beside her, looking out the window and scanning the entirety of her view.

Some time later, and probably far longer than was truly necessary, Janice satisfied herself that there was nothing to see, put her glasses back on the table beside her, and bent over to retrieve a new ball of yarn from the basket beside her chair.

When the street in both directions was entirely empty of both pedestrian and vehicular traffic and Janice Terrin was out of sight in the window across the street, the shadow moved out of Michelle's front yard, across the road, and down the street, turning at the corner of the block and disappearing from view.

Michelle appeared around the corner of the block and walked the last short distance to her house. She opened the front door, went inside, and checked the roast in the oven. It looked perfect and nearly done, so she began to pull out dishes and set the table. Her husband would be home for lunch in ten minutes, and she wanted everything to be ready for him.

As Michelle made the final preparations for lunch, she failed to notice the small bit of dirt that had been tracked onto the runner rug that lay between her dining and living rooms. She didn't know that someone had been in her home just ten minutes earlier. And she didn't know that her pink freshwater pearl necklace was no longer in her jewelry box.

CHAPTER 31

Elnora pushed her fork into her salad and took another bite. She was entirely alone for lunch that day, as Chrissy was out sick and Stan had run home for a quick lunch with his wife. Elnora didn't mind terribly, especially since this particular day she enjoyed the opportunity to be alone with her thoughts.

She hated to admit it, but she felt pretty much the way that characters in movies or books seemed to feel when they first developed a romantic interest. She had always thought it was a bit overblown and fake--how could someone suddenly feel so much better about themselves and literally everything else around them just because they liked someone and that person liked them back? Now, however, Elnora realized that those characters weren't far off. She did feel better about herself and about everything else around her--almost like she now had even more of a reason to try harder and reach for her goals. She felt a very small sense of caution, like she should tread carefully and make sure she really knew Kevin before she gave herself fully to the creation of a relationship. That sense of responsible action was greatly dwarfed by an adolescent-like sense of excitement and anticipation, and the knowledge that if she saw Kevin, heard his voice or even heard someone say his name, her stomach would be flooded with delightful butterflies.

"Does anyone know where Kevin is?" the door to the teacher's lounge was partially open and Brenda, from the front office, had her head inserted through the gap. Elnora looked around at the four other people in the room, who were all shaking their heads, and then turned back to Brenda and also shook her head. "I can't find him anywhere!" Brenda said in exasperation, and then moved back out the door.

Elnora felt the heavy weight of disappointment, because it turned out that hearing Kevin's name hadn't produced the effect she had been certain it would. Instead, she felt curious and a little confused--where *was* Kevin, after all? She had gotten the impression that he didn't come into the teacher's lounge because he had too much to do in his classroom, and therefore simply ate his lunch in his classroom. But if that was the case, Brenda should have been able to find him there. It didn't really make sense for Kevin to go "home" for lunch, since he lived at the inn and didn't have a kitchen. Then again, without a kitchen, it wasn't logical that Kevin could prepare himself a packed lunch either. Maybe he went to the cafe for lunch each day? Elnora shook her head and shrugged lightly to herself, realizing that while she had talked to Kevin for quite a long time by now, there was still a lot that she didn't know about him.

She decided that she wanted to find out, and she was delighted to feel the resulting wave of butterflies in her stomach.

CHAPTER 32

Elnora turned the corner, stepping fully onto Cedar Street, and her heart dropped. There was no familiar shadow waiting at the end of the street, as she had hoped there would be. It was true that she and Kevin hadn't made plans to meet again at a particular time or place, but she definitely felt like she now expected to see him every time she went for her walks. *Hope to see him*, the voice in the back of her mind corrected. Elnora smiled, and suddenly she didn't care whether he was walking with her or not--she felt happy regardless.

As Elnora crossed Main Street and stepped onto the beach, she paused and felt her heart leap in her chest. Just ahead of her, sitting on the sand and facing the ocean, was a shape that had become familiar to her.

"Hi!" Elnora called out joyfully, almost gleefully, and immediately regretted it. She sounded like a thirteen-year-old girl trying to talk casually to her crush and failing miserably.

Kevin turned, smiled, and stood, brushing sand off his pants. "Good afternoon," he responded, grinning widely. It seemed he too was conscious of acting a bit adolescent, because he calmed his impish grin into a softer smile. The butterflies in Elnora's stomach made her feel slightly faint, and she turned and looked out at the ocean.

"Another beautiful day," Elnora said.

"It really is," Kevin acknowledged. He turned and caught her eye, and then waved forward to the beach ahead of them. "Shall we?"

"Of course," Elnora fell into stride beside Kevin, her hand brushing his. The butterflies flurried to a whole new level and Elnora wondered just how much more she could stand.

"Thank goodness it's Friday," Kevin said lightly.

"Oh yeah?" Elnora asked, forcing her eyes up off the sand. "Tiring week?"

"Busy week," Kevin said. "With the exception of an incredibly pleasant, laid-back evening yesterday," he paused for a moment and they both grinned, "I feel like I've been running around, non-stop, all week long."

"Maybe you should make time for breaks," Elnora suggested lightly. "I know you don't feel like you have time for them, with so much still to organize and get done, but sometimes taking a break is worth it because it makes you better able to work harder in a shorter period of time." Elnora genuinely believed what she was telling him, but she wondered for a moment if she really meant to help him by sharing this advice, or if she just wanted to have more time with him each day. *Perhaps it's a little of both*, the voice in the back of her mind told her.

"Funny," Kevin said, dodging a persistent wave that kept on coming and coming toward him, "I've actually had the same thought. Back in McMinnville, I had this one particular class that was loaded with active boys. It was so difficult to get them to focus on their studies, and the harder I pressed them, the worse it became. Then, one day, I had the idea to keep them out in the recess yard for an extra half hour, playing running games. When we came back in, we got more done during our reading period than we ever had before, despite it being half an hour shorter than normal. I continued doing that for the rest of the year, and it was the smartest thing I've ever done as a teacher to handle rambunctious, restless kids."

"I've done the same a few times," Elnora admitted. "So then, you'll start joining us in the lounge for breaks? Or maybe even lunch?" her voice was optimistic, but not, she hoped, pleading.

Kevin shrugged. "I suppose I can pop in for breaks sometimes."

"How about lunch?" Elnora tried again, this time a little more persistently.

Kevin shrugged again, but remained quiet. His face looked more serious than Elnora had ever seen it.

"Where do you usually have lunch?" Elnora asked, trying to keep her voice casual and inquisitive.

"I just grab a sandwich," Kevin said. It sounded like he was making an effort to be casual, but was likely hiding something that he didn't want to say.

"From the cafe?" Elnora hated that she felt so pushy, but she was truly curious, especially since he was acting weirdly.

Kevin nodded, "Yeah, from the cafe."

"But you don't eat there? Where do you eat then? Like today, for example?" Elnora grimaced--she had just shot him with three questions in a row, and he obviously didn't want to talk about it. *But **why**?* she asked herself. Why would anyone have a problem talking about *lunch*, of all things? I mean, it was just *lunch*!

"I usually just walk from the cafe back to the school, and eat while I go," Kevin said. Elnora noted the use of "usually," and the fact that it likely meant it wasn't what he had done that day.

"Huh," Elnora said. She had more questions, lots of them, but forced herself to bite her tongue.

"I'm working on something," Kevin said suddenly, and his voice sounded lighter and more normal. Elnora glanced over at his face and he looked relieved, like he had suddenly figured out how to describe something complex. "During lunch, I'm working on something," Kevin repeated, and his voice was filled with conviction now. "I'm just not ready to talk about it," he explained, looking over at Elnora with a gentle smile on his face.

Elnora returned the soft smile and shrugged. "Oh, okay."

"But I will start coming by during breaks," Kevin said. "I think you're right, it will be good for me."

Elnora smiled more deeply, whether at Kevin or the fresh set of stomach butterflies she wasn't sure.

They continued on, strolling more than walking, as the conversation moved freely and easily from subject to subject. At one point on the way back to town Kevin reached out and gently took hold of Elnora's hand. He didn't say anything, and though she hadn't been expecting it she felt that it was a normal and natural thing to do. She gripped his hand gently but firmly, appreciating its warmth.

When they reached Main Street and stopped to clear the traffic, Kevin turned to Elnora, gently releasing her hand, and made an apologetic face.

"I would love to invite you to my place for some water and conversation," he started, "But I'm afraid I have some things that I absolutely *have* to take care of before tomorrow. Will you accept my apologies and a raincheck for tomorrow evening?"

Elnora smiled, though she couldn't deny that she felt a slight disappointment and she was certain it showed on her face. "Of course," she answered.

Kevin leaned in and kissed her on the cheek, lingering a little longer this time, and then he turned and walked up the west side of the road, probably to cross Main Street closer to the inn.

Elnora watched him for a few seconds before clearing the traffic in both directions and crossing the road, heading east along Cedar Street toward home.

CHAPTER 33

It was 6:00 am on a Saturday morning and Elnora was awake. This wasn't particularly unusual, but what was unusual was that she was walking out of her house at 6:00 am on a Saturday morning. Normally, Elnora spent her Saturday mornings at home, cleaning, organizing and just generally relaxing. Today, however, was a special day. Elnora set down the box in her hands, pulled her keys out of her pocket, and locked her front door. She then picked up the box and carried it to her car, placing it in her trunk before getting in and starting the car.

She drove exactly eleven blocks, pulling up in front of Sandra Feng's house. Sandra was pulling large plastic tables out of her garage, setting them up in parallel along her driveway, and placing white tablecloths over them. Elnora parked her car and stepped out, locking the door and then moving back to the trunk to take out the box.

"Good morning," Elnora said as she approached the driveway. Sandra looked up and smiled at Elnora.

"Good morning."

"How can I help?" Elnora asked, setting her box down on the driveway.

Sandra looked around at the tables and shrugged. "Stephen is posting the signs around town and everyone else is supposed to be here soon, so I think we're pretty much ready to start setting things out."

"Sounds good to me. I suppose we should try to organize things by category?" Elnora asked.

"Yes. Since you're the first one here, just go ahead and choose where you think things should go and everyone else can follow your lead."

"Will do," Elnora said, picking up her box and setting out her donated items on the tables in Sandra's driveway.

By 6:30 am, twenty other women had joined Elnora and Sandra and the tables were full. In fact, some of the items for sale were "displayed" in boxes near the tables where there was no further room left on the tables. Stephen Feng had returned and reported that signs were up along Main Street in both directions, as well as along Cedar Street and some of the other key streets around town. Then he disappeared into the house, probably to return to bed.

Two of the ladies put up a large sign in Sandra's front yard, announcing the Annual Blue Whale Cove Rummage Sale, this year benefitting the Oregon Food Bank--Tillamook location. Finally, satisfied that the items were as well organized as was possible, everyone arranged camp chairs in a large circle on the front lawn, behind the sign, to chat while they waited. Elnora returned to her car to retrieve her camping chair and set it up on the north side of the circle, closest to Sandra's house.

The conversation began as it always did, with casual social banter that allowed everyone to catch up on each other's lives, and then it turned, as it always did, to matters that were more "juicy" and interesting. In this case, unsurprisingly, it was the story of the recent burglaries.

As the discussion evolved, Elnora noted that it became less and less about the details of the recent, reported burglaries and more and more about items that these women had discovered were missing over the past five, ten, and even fifteen years. The first couple of admissions were casual-- one woman had been missing her mother-of-pearl bracelet for the past ten years and another was missing, for the past seven years, the plain gold promise ring her husband had given her when they were high school sweethearts. Then, as more admissions of more missing items were made, the entire group seemed to become excited, as though they were energized by the common bond they had just discovered that they shared.

Elnora, not having anything to contribute to the conversation as she had never personally discovered she was missing anything, listened quietly as the discussion continued to evolve and grow. It was not entirely surprising that the ladies were now considering that they were all the victims of burglaries that had been occurring in the town for many years, and they had never considered it. There had been no obvious signs that someone may have come into and burgled their house; they had simply assumed that they had misplaced, and effectively lost, the item.

The possibility that burglaries had been occurring in Blue Whale Cove for some time, rather than just over the prior two weeks, nearly stunned the group into silence. As they continued to talk, increasingly interrupted by customers coming to make purchases at the sale, Elnora noticed that the tones of voice had turned nervous, and that these women too had experienced a loss of innocence in regards to the town that they thought they knew so well. Several women also expressed concern over the fact that someone in their town, therefore someone they knew and cared for, was dishonest. It was heartbreaking to listen to, because even while they were rightfully upset about the crimes that had been committed against them and others, they were also upset about the fact that someone clearly needed their help, but they didn't know who it was. And they hadn't known for the past … fifteen years. Elnora's affection for the women around her swelled as she heard them echo the sentiments she had voiced to Kevin just a few days earlier. Even though it didn't change the situation, it made her feel better to know that she wasn't alone in wishing she could change it by understanding it better.

By the time the rummage sale ended at noon, they had made over three thousand dollars for the Oregon Food Bank. Perhaps more importantly, they had bonded together more closely than ever, not only because they shared a common complaint, but because they shared a common goal: to find the individual in their town who needed their help.

CHAPTER 34

As the women folded up their camping chairs and moved them to the sidewalk in front of Sandra's house, Elnora helped to box up the few remaining items that hadn't sold at the rummage sale so that they could be donated to Goodwill. She offered to drop them off herself but Sandra said she was leaving in the next few minutes to head down that way, so she would take them. Elnora helped Sandra load the boxes into the back of her SUV, said her goodbyes, and climbed into her car.

Elnora decided to go to the cafe for lunch, rather than running home. She hadn't yet done her weekly grocery shopping and the pantry and fridge were looking rather bare. She knew that she could probably whip something up--a simple sandwich or pesto pasta--but she just didn't feel like it. She felt a sort of nervous excitement; the knowledge that she had quite a few things to get done was tempered by the knowledge that she had a date that evening.

Elnora parked her car in front of the cafe and walked up the steps and through the door. It was still almost an hour until they closed at 1:30, and the place was packed. Elnora didn't recognize anyone she saw sitting in the booths, so she picked a solitary stool by the counter and took a seat.

After several moments, Jeffrey appeared through the door from the kitchen, his hands and arms loaded with plates of food. He saw Elnora sitting at the counter, smiled and winked at her, and went off to deliver his food to a group of tourists sitting in the big corner booth. After ensuring they had everything they needed, he returned behind the counter and walked over to Elnora.

"What a pleasant surprise," Jeffrey said, placing a glass of ice water in front of Elnora. "The usual?"

Elnora shook her head. "Actually, I was hoping for a big bowl of your famous clam chowder."

Jeffrey raised his eyebrows at her. "Really?" Elnora nodded. "Okay, clam chowder it is." As he made his way back toward the kitchen, he stopped and checked on several patrons sitting at the counter. Everyone smiled and nodded, and Jeffrey hurried off.

Elnora looked around the cafe again, surprised that with the place filled to capacity, she didn't recognize anyone. Jeffrey appeared suddenly, placing a large bowl of steaming soup in front of her.

"Bon appetit!" Jeffrey said, sliding a napkin of cutlery toward her.

Elnora smiled, "Thank you--it looks delicious!" and Jeffrey winked again before moving back down the counter and out onto the main floor. His three wait staff employees were also busy, checking on patrons and refilling drinks. Elnora slid her big soup spoon through the creamy white soup and tried it, relishing the warmth and mixture of flavors. It was creamy and thick, but not so creamy that it blocked all other flavors and not so thick that you felt you had to chew it. There were a few chewy clams, but also some small diced potatoes, carrots and even a few peas. It was delicious, and Elnora considered that she may need a second bowl.

Elnora was halfway through her soup when suddenly half the patrons in the cafe stood, almost simultaneously, and left. Elnora turned and saw them standing around together in a big group in the parking lot, in front of and around various cars.

"Big family road trip," Jeffrey said from behind Elnora.

Elnora turned and looked at him. "Huge family road trip," she corrected and he nodded.

"It's good for business," Jeffrey said, shrugging. "They told me they stop here every time they pass through--every five years--but the truth is I don't remember them ever coming before."

"Well families grow and change," Elnora pointed out.

"True," Jeffrey nodded. "So," he took a deep breath and sighed, "Now that I can finally take a break and catch my breath, tell me--how have you been?"

"Good," Elnora said, continuing to eat her soup. "This is amazing, by the way," Elnora said, indicating to the soup.

"Secret recipe," Jeffrey said, and winked at her again.

Elnora smiled. "I may have to steal that from you," she teased.

"I'd like to see you try," Jeffrey teased back and they both laughed. "So … everything good at the school?" Jeffrey asked, raising his eyebrows and looking at her. "Nothing new to report?"

"What do you know?" Elnora asked, scraping the remainder of the soup from the bottom of her bowl.

"Nothing," Jeffrey said, clearing the bowl from the counter and placing it in a dish bin under the counter.

"Come on, Jeffrey, *someone* obviously told you *something*," Elnora pressed.

"Only good things," Jeffrey offered, grabbing a hand towel and wiping down a non-existent mess on the counter.

"What good things?" Elnora asked.

"Nothing really, just that you may have found a special someone," Jeffrey said lightly.

Elnora gasped in genuine surprise. "Who told you that?" Jeffrey made as if to move away. "Jeffrey? Who told you that?"

Jeffrey shrugged his shoulders. "Chrissy was in here the other day," he finally revealed. "She told me that you're dating the new teacher in town," he smiled, a warm, friendly smile.

Elnora politely returned the smile, but shook her head. "Not really dating," she explained, and watched Jeffrey's face fall, "But certainly enjoying my time getting to know him," she added. In the back of her head she made a note that she had to talk with Chrissy. It was unlike her to put rumors on the gossip mill in town, especially about Elnora. They usually protected one another from the gossip.

"Well maybe that's how she put it," Jeffrey said, scratching the whiskers on his chin. "She didn't quite seem herself--a little preoccupied, you know?"

Elnora nodded thoughtfully. It was far more likely that Chrissy made a passing statement that lumped her and Kevin together, and then Jeffrey drew his own conclusions. Nonetheless, she was definitely going to ask Chrissy about it over tea the next day.

"I wouldn't be surprised if it was all the burglaries," Jeffrey continued. "They seem to be upsetting everyone in town."

"All the burglaries?" Elnora asked.

"Well yes," Jeffrey said. "Now that residents are talking about reporting things that have gone missing over the years, it looks like there have been over fifty burglaries in the last fifteen or so years."

Elnora gaped. "Is Chief Hinson actually allowing theft reports for all that?"

Jeffrey shrugged. "Why wouldn't he?"

"Well I'm just wondering if there's proof that all these things have been stolen," Elnora said.

"There's no proof they haven't been," Jeffrey said, "And it's definitely strange that so many people in the same town would have so many items just go 'missing,' don't you think?" Elnora nodded--she couldn't disagree that it did seem suspicious. She just hadn't realized that the discussion she had witnessed over the last few hours wasn't the first such discussion in town, and that other residents had already become alert to the fact that there may be a sinister reason behind the missing items they had previously thought were lost over the years.

"It's just so …" Elnora stopped, struggling to find the right word. "Sudden. As if three burglaries weren't enough to contend with, now we're talking about how there might actually be fifty? Poor Chief Hinson," she added.

A patron at the end of the counter caught Jeffrey's eye and he stood and turned. "I guess you never know what can happen," he said as he started to move away.

Elnora smiled, "No, you don't. Thanks for the soup."

Jeffrey threw her another wink and then turned away.

Elnora left money on the counter and then went back out to her car. She drove straight south, to Tillamook and her weekly grocery shopping.

CHAPTER 35

Elnora had just finished checking all the windows and doors around the house when someone knocked at her front door. She opened it and found Kevin standing on her front porch, holding two paper bags of groceries.

"I'm sorry to presume," Kevin said, smiling over the groceries, "But I was hoping I could cook you dinner tonight. After our walk," he added.

Elnora smiled. "Wow. That's … lovely of you," Elnora pushed her door all the way open, indicating for Kevin to come in.

"Thank you. I figured we should use your place," Kevin set the groceries down on the kitchen counter, "Since I don't have a kitchen."

Elnora laughed lightly. "Smart. Do you want me to help you put things in the fridge?" she asked.

Kevin shook his head. "If you don't mind, I'll take care of that, while you go put on your shoes."

"Okay," Elnora said and moved off to the living room. She quickly slipped on her shoes and tied them, listening to the sounds of Kevin moving around in her kitchen. Finally, just as she finished, she heard the refrigerator door close.

"Okay," Kevin said, coming back into view. "All set. Ready?"

Elnora nodded. "Yep."

They stepped out the front door and Elnora locked it behind them, before heading off down the street. Kevin took Elnora's hand almost immediately and they strolled slowly through town, admiring the quaint houses and neat yards. The town was quiet and beautiful in the early evening, and as they approached 1st Street, Elnora slowed to a stop, pulling Kevin to a stop beside her.

"Is everything alright?" Kevin asked, looking at Elnora.

Elnora nodded. "I was just thinking," she paused and looked at him, "What if we stayed in town tonight? Walked the streets?"

"Sounds good to me," Kevin said, "As long as I'm with you, it's a good night," he gently squeezed her hand.

Elnora blushed and squeezed back. They turned and walked north on 1st Street, alternating between casual conversation and comfortable silence. When they approached the final block to the north, they turned east down Redwood Street and walked to 2nd Street, again turning right so they were heading back south.

By the time they reached the southernmost end of 2nd Street, they were both breathing a little more heavily. Elnora glanced down at the watch on her wrist and noticed that they had been walking for more than an hour and a half. Her hand was sweaty where it clung to Kevin's, but she didn't want to let go. They looked at each other, nodded in silent agreement, and turned back north, to Cedar Street and Elnora's home.

Half an hour later Elnora sat at her kitchen table, watching Kevin work in her kitchen. He seemed completely comfortable and perfectly oriented, knowing precisely where to look to find whatever tools he needed. Kevin credited Elnora for this--he told her that she had organized her kitchen in a very functional and logical way. Elnora accepted the compliment, while making sure he knew that it hadn't been on purpose. She considered herself useful in the kitchen, but far from skilled. Kevin assured her that he was the same, but when he set her plate of mahi-mahi tacos in front of her, Elnora knew he was just being humble.

They enjoyed a quiet dinner--another sign that the food was incredible and delicious--and then Elnora helped Kevin clean the kitchen and wash and put away the dishes. They moved into the living room, sitting on Elnora's couch with cups of chamomile tea, where they continued to talk easily and comfortably.

As time moved from late afternoon into early evening and beyond, and they both grew increasingly tired, their voices became quieter and slower. Finally, Kevin leaned forward in a motion that clearly meant he was thinking of leaving. Elnora resisted the urge to protest out loud, though she was certain it wouldn't have bothered him had she uttered the, "No!" that rose into her throat.

Once again, Kevin made his gentlemanly apologies, thanking Elnora for the lovely evening and plainly stating his hope that they could do it again soon. Elnora agreed whole-heartedly, though she noticed that her words were beginning to slur and she had to focus harder than usual in order to move her body effectively.

Kevin grabbed his light jacket off the back of the couch and slipped it on, then went over to the entryway and slipped on his tennis shoes, reaching down to tie them. He stood and unlocked and opened the door, looking out into the misty town for a moment before turning back to her. Without a word, he leaned forward and kissed her gently, his lips barely brushing hers. Then he turned and walked off, down her driveway and to the street.

He didn't turn back to look at her, but Elnora knew that he was smiling, just as she was.

CHAPTER 36

Elnora woke up to the sun streaming in through her bedroom window. It was 8:00 am, which was late for her. She knew immediately that if she did her normal hike out to the point at Cape Lookout, there was a chance she would miss lunch at the cafe. As soon as the thought crossed her mind, however, she dismissed it. She would far rather miss lunch than her weekly hike, especially on such a beautiful day. She quickly showered and dressed and then stepped into the kitchen for a light breakfast of fresh grapefruit.

After setting her empty bowl and cutlery into the sink, Elnora opened her pantry cabinet to grab some trail mix for the hike. The bag had been pushed to the back of the cabinet, and as she pulled it forward, a small, velvet blue box came with it, hitting first the counter and then the floor. Elnora stared at it in surprise for a moment. She knew what the box held--the sterling silver spoon engraved with her name and birthdate that her grandmother had given her when she was born. She just didn't understand what it was doing in the pantry--she kept it in her "china" cabinet--one cabinet devoted to the lovely kitchenware items that she didn't use, but rather just looked at every once in awhile.

Elnora shrugged her shoulders lightly and then reached down to pick up the box. It was incredibly light. Too light. Elnora pulled the top off, revealing an empty interior. The next minute seemed to drag on for ten, as Elnora's mind raced. She didn't feel terribly upset about the missing spoon--after all, she never used it and she would never sell it--she just felt confused. Where had it gone? She pushed things around in the pantry cabinet and then removed every item, but the spoon wasn't there. She checked her china cabinet, also carefully removing every item, but the spoon wasn't there either. She worked through the rest of her kitchen, checking every drawer and cabinet, and couldn't find the spoon anywhere.

Finally, Elnora came to the conclusion that the spoon was definitely missing. And considering that she was absolutely certain that it had been in the kitchen, the box was still in the kitchen, and she hadn't taken the spoon out and moved it anywhere, a seed of doubt had been slowly growing in her mind.

Perhaps it too, like many other items in town, had been taken.

CHAPTER 37

Elnora pulled into the parking lot for the Cape Lookout trail and noticed Kevin's car immediately. She felt a surge of almost frantic energy--a desire to go running down the trail and into Kevin's arms. It was one thing to feel that there was a burglar among the residents in her town, but quite another to suspect that she herself was a victim. She wanted something comfortable and familiar, and right now Kevin felt like that to her.

Elnora managed to calm herself enough to remove her backpack from the trunk of her car and ensure that her car was fully locked before she headed down the trail. She also managed to keep herself from running--after all, it was about two miles out to the point, and if she had to go that far to find Kevin she certainly wouldn't be able to run the entire way--but she was definitely walking the trail much faster than she ever had before.

Where Elnora's mind normally wandered over a variety

of topics as she hiked this trail, today she marveled over the fact that all she could think about was talking with Kevin, as if she hadn't had her fill the night before. Elnora had once dated a nervous young man who had speculated that long-term couples must eventually run out of things to say. She had understood his point of view, after all a lot of the initial talking that couples did was back story--filling in the details of their lives up to that point. But on the other hand, she had never had any difficulty finding things to talk about with friends and family members--why should it be any different with a significant other? Elnora herself had never dated anyone who made her feel the way Kevin did--like she wanted to talk to and listen to him indefinitely. Especially when she felt a little anxious or bothered by something, he had a way of calming her down, without making her feel silly or self-conscious and without making less of her concerns.

Elnora came around a bend in the trail and her heart leapt--Kevin was walking a mere thirty yards ahead of her. She pulled in a deep breath in order to call out to him and then stopped, freezing in her tracks. Kevin had stopped suddenly in the middle of the trail, as if to listen. Elnora silently stepped to the side, behind a tree, as Kevin turned to look around, his motions furtive and suspicious. A group of hikers appeared on the trail in front of them, hiking in their direction, and Kevin immediately straightened, lengthening and straightening his back as though stretching. He nodded as the hikers passed him, and then turned and watched as they moved farther down the trail. Elnora moved further behind the tree, trying to remain out of sight from both Kevin and the hikers heading in her direction. As they moved past her, Elnora realized she was holding her breath and let it out slowly and quietly.

Finally, the sound of footsteps faded into silence and

Elnora carefully looked around the tree. She caught a glimpse of just the back of Kevin as he stepped off the trail and disappeared into the forest. She paused for a moment, debating. Part of her wanted to follow him, but an even bigger part of her was afraid of what she might learn if she did. The former part won out, and she moved quickly down the trail to where Kevin had disappeared into the woods. She was almost positive that it was exactly the same spot where she had watched him move off the trail the week before.

Elnora hesitated before stepping off the trail. While she couldn't see Kevin, she could see slight impressions in the earth where he had stepped, and she was fairly certain that she could hear his footsteps above the distant sound of crashing waves. The ferns that covered the ground were damp with moisture, and after a few moments Elnora could tell that her pants were becoming soaked. She tried to pick her steps more carefully, working around the larger ferns, but it was impossible to avoid them all.

Finally, the undergrowth thinned out and Elnora came to a sort of clearing. It wasn't entirely devoid of tall cedar trees, but they were sparse enough that sunlight was able to reach the forest floor. Just ahead of her, the earth dropped away and the sound of crashing waves was almost deafening. Elnora stayed well back and glanced around the open space. There was no sign of Kevin, and no further impressions in the earth to follow. There was, however, a small ring of stones on the ground in the center of the trees. Elnora approached cautiously, but they were nothing but large beach stones, polished smooth by the ocean waves. She wondered what they were doing up here, several hundred feet above the ocean, and she glanced around again. Even as her eyes passed around the trees surrounding her, Kevin moved out from behind the largest one, a soft smile on his face.

Elnora felt a surge of confusion and wariness and stepped back a few paces. Kevin stepped forward a couple of feet and stopped.

"You found my secret place," Kevin said, and smiled again.

"What do you mean?" Elnora asked, her voice thick and low. "What is this place?" She looked around the clearing and then back at him, her eyes pleading for him to make this all okay, to make things the way they were.

Kevin waved his arms around, first at the general space and then at the stones on the forest floor. "This is Aunt Sam's memorial," he explained.

Confusion remained on Elnora's face, although now it had brightened subtly, as if someone had turned on a light nearby.

"She didn't want to be buried," Kevin said. "She said she refused to spend eternity in a box in the ground," he smiled at the memory. "She asked to be cremated, and her ashes scattered someplace beautiful." Kevin looked around him. "I couldn't think of a better spot than here. And this way," he added, "I can still visit her."

Elnora nodded, wanting to believe him. He sounded sincere, but …

"Why are you being so sneaky about it?"

"You're not supposed to step off trail. But I couldn't very well memorialize her on the trail--she would complain about the traffic," again he smiled in memory.

"Why didn't we ever meet? All those times you came to Blue Whale Cove to visit her, and I never saw you or never heard of you? Samantha loved to talk, about everything and everyone. I remember, she told wonderful stories," the doubts that Elnora had been harboring suddenly came pouring out of her, and she felt all the better for having finally released them.

Kevin took a few steps closer. "But never about herself," he said.

Elnora opened her mouth to protest and then stopped. Thinking back through all the times Samantha had shared stories with her, Elnora couldn't recall a single time the stories had been about Samantha herself. Elnora looked up at Kevin, a new question in her eyes.

"You're right, she loved to gossip. She said it made her feel alive. But she never spread gossip about herself."

Elnora nodded in agreement. "You're right, I can't remember her ever talking about herself. Not once. But I still can't believe we never saw you, though. That you never left the house together whenever you came to visit."

"She was sick, Elnora," Kevin explained.

Elnora gasped and shook her head, trying to fight the news even though she knew deep down that it was true.

"She was HIV positive. She didn't tell anyone because in her own eyes, it was a mortifying embarrassment. She grew up in a time when being HIV positive meant an association to dirty and very unladylike interactions with others. She took her medication to manage it, and her brother, my father, came out to check on her every month--make sure she was taking her medication and going in for her regular tests. That's when I came to visit her, and that's why she never told anyone." Kevin paused, seeing the light dawn in Elnora's eyes.

"To admit that her brother and nephew came to town every month or so would potentially open the door to the question 'Why?' and that was a question she could never answer."

Kevin nodded.

"Poor Samantha," Elnora said quietly.

Kevin shrugged. "She wasn't in a lot of pain," he said, "Until the very end. My dad found out that she'd been taking magnesium tablets and flushing her real medication down the toilet for more than six months."

Elnora took a deep, gasping breath, tears forming in her eyes.

"Her only explanation was that she hated the side effects. Unfortunately, when we got her in to the doctor for a full battery of tests, we discovered that the virus had spread and exacerbated, and there was nothing that could be done," Kevin shrugged again, his voice and gaze distant. "She seemed content with her fate, like it was a way for her to start over, on her terms. She died in her sleep, much more quickly than we had expected," Kevin's voice cracked and his eyes were watery. "But then, that was Aunt Sam--she always did do things her own way," he fell into silence, looking out into the distance and the view of the ocean in between the trees.

"I'm so sorry," Elnora said sincerely, stepping forward to place a hand on Kevin's arm. He smiled at her, remaining silent.

They stood there together for awhile, breathing deeply the mixed ocean and forest air. Finally, Kevin turned toward her.

"Now that I'm back in the area, I try to come out every week. I like to just stand here, enjoy the view, and remember." They stood quietly together for a few minutes, doing exactly that. Finally, Kevin turned toward Elnora, a question in his eyes. "Would you come with me to visit her sometimes?" His voice was small and childlike; hopeful.

"I'd like that," Elnora said.

Kevin took her hand and squeezed it gently, then retrieved his large backpack from beside a tree and put it onto his back. He led Elnora through the ferns and back to the trail, stopping to make sure no one was coming before they came out of the forest. On the trail, Kevin paused and looked at her.

"Do you want to continue out to the point?" he asked, and Elnora nodded, and then shrugged.

"Do you? You haven't already been?" she asked.

Kevin shook his head. "Yes I do, and no I haven't."

They walked on together, sharing stories of Kevin's Aunt Sam. When they reached the point they fell into silence, admiring the view and enjoying each other's company. After they had stood there for several minutes, Kevin took a deep breath.

"I'm trying to buy her house."

"Samantha's?" Elnora clarified and Kevin nodded.

"She actually willed it to me, but when it came down to it, we had to sell it to handle some medical bills. The couple that's there now," he looked to Elnora as though he thought she may be able to fill in the names, but she only shrugged--she didn't actually know who lived in Samantha's old house, "They have been considering selling it for awhile. They agreed not to put it on the market yet, and we've been in negotiations since I arrived." He paused and looked over at Elnora. "That's why I haven't always been available at lunch time or in the evenings--I meet them whenever they can."

Elnora nodded in understanding. "And how is it going?"

"Well, I think. They were asking a fair price, but they just had a lot of interesting conditions. Some of them are a little odd--like they want to stay in the house until we close, but they're willing to pay for the home inspector and closing cost fees in exchange, but then they want to use an inspector they know, but he's not showing up on any lists as a licensed inspector. You know, weird stuff. I'm glad Anna knows what she's doing, because I'd be lost and probably giving up all sorts of rights," Kevin shrugged and then stepped around a particularly large mud puddle, turning back and offering Elnora his hand. She took it and walked around the puddle balanced on her tiptoes.

"Anna is good," Elnora agreed. "She helped me a lot when I bought my place--saved me over five grand in various fees."

Kevin nodded. "I'm hoping she'll do the same for me. I didn't realize how many fees are associated with buying a house," Kevin said, giving an exasperated sigh. "I knew about the down payment, but that was it. The taxes and other fees--I may have to live without furniture for awhile," he laughed and Elnora giggled.

"That's exciting though," Elnora said. "The house is over on 4th Street, isn't it?" Elnora was digging through her memories--she had only gone to Samantha's house a couple of times, as Samantha much preferred bringing her baked goods to others' homes.

"Yes, just north of Cedar Street. Not far from your place," Kevin reached over and took Elnora's hand. She smiled at him, and he smiled back, and they turned together to walk back east, into the woods, past Samantha Hiller's memorial and to the parking lot.

Kevin walked with Elnora to her car, finally releasing her hand so that she could remove her backpack and place it in the trunk. As she stepped over to the driver's door, unlocked it and pulled it open, Kevin cleared his throat.

"I have to meet Anna to go over some proposed negotiations on the sale," he paused and rolled his eyes, and then smiled at her, "But if you're available for dinner, I'd like to treat you. Perhaps at the inn restaurant?"

"That sounds fine. I have a standing 'tea date' with Chrissy in an hour anyway," Elnora said.

"Perfect. Shall we say five o'clock at the restaurant?" Kevin asked, and then added, "I would offer to pick you up and drive you there, like a proper gentleman, but I'm afraid that once you see the entirely unglamorous interior of my car you won't like me very much anymore."

Elnora laughed. "I'm sure that's not true, but just to ease your mind I'll gladly meet you at the restaurant."

Kevin smiled, then paused. Elnora's heart began to race and her belly filled with butterflies. Kevin leaned forward and gently pressed his lips against hers, and then gave her a throaty "Bye" before heading over to his own car.

Elnora got into the driver's seat and shut the door, but didn't start the car immediately. She heard Kevin's car start up and watched as he backed out of his spot and then pulled forward, pausing to wave at her before driving out of the lot, turning north on the road. Finally, after what seemed an eternity of blissful silence, Elnora started her car, pulled out of the spot, and followed in Kevin's wake.

CHAPTER 38

When Elnora reached town, she didn't spend a single second worrying about whether she could catch Jeffrey in time to have lunch at the cafe. She didn't even feel hungry, but she drove straight home and prepared a salad with shredded turkey, slivered carrots and sliced cucumbers. She forced herself to eat two big bites and then she couldn't force herself to eat any more. She simply wasn't hungry and it didn't bother her at all.

After covering her barely-touched salad with plastic wrap and placing it in the fridge for later, Elnora went into her bathroom and brushed her teeth and then grabbed her keys and stepped out her front door. She pulled it firmly shut and locked it behind her, cutting across the lawn to the sidewalk and heading north to Chrissy's house. She walked slowly--not only was she a bit earlier than usual, she also wanted to calm herself so that she wouldn't blurt her heart out in the first moment after arriving. She was used to telling Chrissy just about anything and everything that was going on in her life, but the truth was that she wasn't quite ready to tell Chrissy all about Kevin. For one, it was still so brand new, and also she enjoyed savoring the "secret" of her feelings.

By the time she arrived at Chrissy's door, Elnora had come up with a couple things she could talk to Chrissy about, but she still felt that there was a decent chance she would accidentally spill the beans about how much time she had spent with Kevin over the last week, and how much she really liked him.

Elnora took a deep breath and knocked on Chrissy's door. Seconds passed, then a full minute, and there was no answer. Elnora frowned and glanced down at the watch on her wrist. 1:47 p.m. She was a little earlier than usual, but not by much--only about eight to ten minutes or so. Chrissy's car was in the driveway, so Elnora was fairly certain she was home. She knocked again, and this time she heard a distant thump. It sounded like something fairly heavy--at least fifty pounds, had been placed roughly down on the floor.

"Chrissy?" Elnora called out, mildly alarmed. Another thump. "Chrissy?" Elnora called again.

Silence. And then …

"Just a second! Coming!" Chrissy's voice was muffled, and Elnora wondered if she was in the bathroom.

Another two minutes passed, and then Elnora heard Chrissy's feet crossing the floor. The deadbolt slid back from the lock and Chrissy pulled the door open, a slightly frazzled smile on her face.

"You're early!" Chrissy said, waving Elnora into the house.

"A little," Elnora admitted. She noted that Chrissy was breathing rapidly and turned toward her friend. "Are you okay?"

Chrissy smiled widely. "Of course! But I'm afraid I haven't set the table for tea yet. Surprise, surprise, right?"

Elnora smiled and followed her friend into the kitchen. "Yes, totally shocking," she agreed. She stopped in the entryway, her eyes on the light over the kitchen table. Or rather, what was hanging on delicate fish wire just below the light. It was a large, colorful, blown-glass jellyfish-- just like the ones she had seen in the window of Blue Whale Cove Treasures.

"Isn't it pretty?" Chrissy asked, grabbing mugs and saucers out of a cabinet.

"It is," Elnora admitted. Though the jellyfish's placement below the light was awkward at best, the position also flooded the bell with light that shone all the way down to the tips of the tentacles. The effect was nothing short of mesmerizing--the colorful glass seemed to be emitting light rather than simply reflecting it.

"I picked it up at Treasures yesterday," Chrissy said, placing the mugs and saucers on the table and returning to the kitchen to fill the kettle. Elnora followed her into the kitchen, grabbing the honey and the tea caddy and bringing them over to the table.

"It's very nice," Elnora acknowledged again.

"I know, I know, it's not really 'useful,'" Chrissy said, placing the kettle on the stove and turning on the burner. "But," Chrissy paused, "It's so pretty!" she said again.

Elnora smiled and took a seat at the table, watching as Chrissy did the same.

"So," Chrissy said, a twinkle in her brown eyes, "Anything new and exciting to report?"

"My silver spoon is missing," Elnora blurted out. It was one of the things she had considered saying on her walk over, though she hadn't meant to blurt it out so guiltily. Not surprisingly, Chrissy looked surprised.

"What?" Chrissy asked, glancing up at the jellyfish.

"My silver baby spoon--you know, the one engraved with my name and birthdate?" Elnora paused and Chrissy nodded. "It's missing. But just the spoon--the box was still in the cabinet. Not the right cabinet," Elnora realized she was babbling, but she didn't care. It was relieving to share the news. Chrissy remained silent. "It was in the pantry cabinet. I think … well actually, I'm pretty sure it must have been taken." Elnora chose "taken" over "stolen," figuring it would be softer for her hyper-sensitive and nervous friend.

"Why?" Chrissy asked, standing up and walking into the kitchen. She seemed to have forgotten why she went there, however, as she stood in the center of the space, looking around.

"Because I searched everywhere for it, and I cannot figure out how it could be gone, but the box still here. Not only still here, but shoved in the back of the pantry instead of in the china cabinet where I left it," Elnora said matter-of-factly.

The kettle began to whistle and Chrissy turned, reaching out and shutting off the burner. "You never used it, right?" she said, turning and grabbing a potholder out of a drawer. "And you would never sell it," she turned toward the kettle.

"Of course not," Elnora answered.

"So at least it's not a terrible loss," Chrissy said simply.

Elnora paused, surprised by the curtness in her friend's tone. She had expected her friend to become anxious and nervous, but this almost sounded like she didn't care at all. "I guess," Elnora admitted. "But it's not a great loss, either." Chrissy nodded in understanding and moved to pull the kettle off the stove. The potholder slipped and the kettle fell forward, splashing hot water onto the floor. Chrissy jumped back out of the way, avoiding the worst of the splash but getting some water spots on her shirt and pants.

"Shoot!" Chrissy exclaimed, looking down at her clothes.

"Are you okay?" Elnora stood and grabbed the hand towel from the stove handle and threw it onto the water on the floor.

Chrissy nodded. "I'm okay," she said, looking down at her wet clothes. She grabbed another hand towel and helped Elnora clean up the water on the floor. She picked up and refilled the kettle and set it back on the stove, turning the burner back on. "I'm going to go change," she said, and Elnora nodded.

Elnora heard Chrissy's bedroom door close and she turned to the table, her eyes drawn back to the jellyfish. She had to admit that Chrissy was right: it definitely was a very pretty thing. Elnora's mind caught, and she involuntarily sucked in a breath. Her eyes moved around the kitchen, and then the living room. Chrissy may not have had many decorations, but those that she did have were all pretty things.

Elnora moved out of the kitchen, through the living room and into the hallway leading to the bedrooms and bathroom. She could hear Chrissy moving around in her room, opening and closing drawers and the closet. Elnora opened her mouth to call out to Chrissy, and then noticed that the door to the spare bedroom was slightly ajar. She placed her hand on the door knob and started to pull the door closed, but then curiosity overtook her and she pushed it gently open, wondering just how huge a mess Chrissy was hiding. However, the small crack she had created revealed no mess whatsoever. Elnora pushed the door harder, opening it fully.

The room was spotless. And completely empty. There was not one piece of furniture, nor one bit of dust anywhere.

Elnora was certain that if she wiped a tissue over the window sill and baseboards it would come back clean. The pine wood floors were polished to a glossy shine and she could tell that they had been swept recently.

Elnora felt both enormous relief, as well as crushing confusion. Why would Chrissy keep this room closed if it was empty? She had always said it was closed and locked because she would be embarrassed if anyone ever saw it--was she embarrassed that it was empty? Did she simply feel that she couldn't afford to furnish it as a nice guest room? Elnora shook her head. It just didn't make any sense at all. She stepped into the room, past the small wall that bordered the edge of the closet, and saw it.

Suddenly, Elnora was aware of just how silent the house was. She could hear Chrissy moving around in her bedroom--she was taking an awfully long time to change her clothes--but there were no other noises. Even the compressor for the refrigerator in the kitchen seemed to have shut off. Elnora closed her eyes and fought back the urge to simply turn on her heels and walk out of the room, closing the door behind her and forgetting everything she suddenly suspected. Things would just go back to the way they were, and that was okay, wasn't it?

Elnora opened her eyes and stared down at the hope chest she hadn't seen in twenty years. It was smaller than it was in her memory--she remembered it being as big as a twin bed--but it was still fairly large: at least three feet tall, two feet wide and five feet long. She stuck her foot out, trying to nudge it, and it didn't move. She bent down to lift it and it still wouldn't budge. She wasn't sure if the chest was heavier than she could manage or if it was bolted to the floor, possibly both. She bent to try again when the bedroom door behind her was pushed forcefully, loudly banging into the wall. Elnora started and stood, turning to face her friend.

Chrissy was pale, her eyes wide with horror. "What are you doing?" her breath came in ragged gasps, as though she had been running, but Elnora knew it was just the beginning of an anxiety attack.

"The door was ajar," Elnora began, her heart pounding in her chest. "I went to close it for you and I accidentally hit the door with my fist, causing it to swing open," Elnora's stomach tightened at the lie, but she muscled past it. "The room is spotless, Chrissy, why are you so worried about it?"

Chrissy's eyes flew to the hope chest on the floor beside her friend and she moved over toward it, standing in front of it defensively. "I cleaned it up," she said, unconvincingly. "I've been working on it for weeks … months … and I finally got it cleaned yesterday."

"Then why are you so upset right now?" Elnora asked, her voice soft and gentle. "I'm not seeing a mess, I'm seeing a spotless room. There's nothing here."

"*Everything's* here," Chrissy breathed, and then clamped her hand over her mouth, her face clearly displaying the shock she felt.

Elnora's heart dropped further, and she glanced down at the chest. "What's in the chest, Chrissy?" Elnora asked, certain she didn't actually want to hear the answer.

"All of my messy stuff," Chrissy said immediately, a response that had clearly been rehearsed.

"You're guarding it from me," Elnora pointed out, and Chrissy moved to walk away but couldn't--it was as though her feet were cemented to the floor. "I don't think you'd care if it was just messy stuff. Please let me see," Elnora said.

Chrissy shook her head, acting more like a petulant child than an adult protecting her right to privacy.

"I need you to open the chest, Chrissy," Elnora replied, amazed at how much calmer her voice sounded than she felt. Chrissy tried to shrug nonchalantly, but it came out stiff and unconvincing.

"I lost the key years ago," Chrissy's voice was weak, and she cleared her throat as though to make her voice stronger. "You know that."

"It's too heavy for that to be true," Elnora said simply, with absolutely no way to prove that it hadn't been that empty when Chrissy lost the key--if she had ever lost the key.

"It's just papers and junk," Chrissy tried.

"Please open the chest, Chrissy," Elnora repeated, watching her friend. She was prepared for the defensive anger that she was sure would come, but what her friend did next caught her completely by surprise. Chrissy crumpled to the floor like a ragdoll, her body wracked with deep, gasping sobs. Elnora rushed forward, kneeling on the floor and pulling her friend into a tight hug. "Breathe, Chrissy, just breathe," Elnora urged. Chrissy shook her head and continued to sob.

They sat there together, on the floor in Chrissy's spare bedroom, Chrissy clinging to Elnora desperately as she sobbed and sobbed. Elnora held her friend, feeling her relief as she rid herself of years of anxiety and secrets. Finally, Chrissy's breathing calmed and her sobs became just an occasional sharp gasp of air. Elnora stood, pulling Chrissy up with her, and walked with her into the living room, sitting Chrissy down on the couch. Elnora grabbed a tissue from the box on the coffee table and wiped the tears from her friend's face, eliciting a shaky smile that was heart-wrenchingly raw.

"Are you ready?" Elnora finally asked, her voice soft and gentle.

A shadow of fear passed before Chrissy's eyes and her

breathing quickened. She closed her eyes and forced deep breaths, then finally nodded, opened her eyes, and looked at her friend.

Elnora listened quietly as Chrissy explained how she first began having strong anxiety attacks, and a compulsive feeling that she needed to have something--something that would make her really happy--in order to stop them, when she was thirteen. She had told her mom, who had explained puberty to her, and all the changes therein. Chrissy had then assumed that what she was experiencing was normal, and she dealt with it for two years. Then, at fifteen, around the time she began to suspect that not everyone experienced puberty in the same way she was experiencing it, Chrissy's first crush began dating someone else. Elnora remembered this time--it was the first time she could recall her friend having a full-blown anxiety attack, with panicked, rapid breathing and cool, clammy skin. As soon as Chrissy found out, she ran home and into her parent's room, climbing under the covers on her mother's side of the bed and sobbing into the pillow. Gradually, her breathing calmed and she came out from under the covers, looking around at the quiet room. Her eyes fell on her mother's jewelry chest, and the delicate white gold necklace with the teardrop emerald hanging from it. Chrissy loved that necklace and always begged to wear it, but her mother rarely let her try it on, and she never let her take it from the house.

Chrissy had moved carefully out of the bed and pulled the necklace from the jewelry chest, carefully undoing the clasp and placing it around her neck. The cool touch of the chain and gem calmed Chrissy instantly and she went to her bedroom, putting on her best dress and admiring herself in the tall mirror on the back of her door. Then her mother had come home and Chrissy had panicked, removing the necklace and hiding it in her underwear drawer. She managed to get the necklace back into the jewelry chest the next morning, while her mom cooked breakfast and her dad took his shower, and no one had noticed or mentioned anything.

As time went on, Chrissy moved through borrowing various pieces of jewelry her parents had every time she had an anxiety attack. At some point, these items no longer satisfied her and she started to think about the pretty things that others had. Her intention had always been to just borrow them, but as time went on she discovered that if she kept pretty things to hand, she could look at them whenever she wanted. Unfortunately, holding onto the items didn't abate her desire for more, and so she had felt forced to continue "borrowing".

Chrissy tried to soften the damage by taking things that weren't used or were even packed away. And it had worked for a long time for her--she had collected many items over the years without anyone being the wiser to it. But in the last two weeks the anxiety had ratcheted up to a whole new level and Chrissy had begun making mistakes. They were costly mistakes--ones that alerted the town and increased the residents' vigilance. And in the meantime, her anxiety had continued to climb.

Elnora let her friend talk, without interrupting, until she had said everything she needed to say. Finally, Chrissy turned to her with sad eyes, her shoulders hunched forward as though she were prepared for the reprimand she was certain would come. Instead, Elnora reached out and placed her hand on her friend's knee.

"Why didn't you tell me--or anyone--about the anxiety?" Elnora asked, her voice laced with the pain she felt for her friend's suffering.

Chrissy shrugged. "I felt like I couldn't," she said simply. "I felt like it was something everyone goes through and has to deal with, and so I needed to just face it and figure it out. But I've just been so scared for so long about everything."

Elnora reached out and pulled Chrissy into a tight hug. "I wish you'd told me," she said, but her voice wasn't chastising her friend, it was simply sad. "Of course it's normal to feel some anxiety or stress occasionally, but not all the time. And certainly not about everything."

Chrissy nodded, and a fresh round of tears started running down her face. "I just didn't know what to do," her voice cracked, "So I followed others--mostly you. You seemed to know exactly what you wanted to do, and you were so happy. So when you joined the cheer squad, I joined the cheer squad. When you joined the track team, I joined the track team. You signed up for cooking club, I signed up for cooking club," the tears were coming harder now, and Chrissy's voice was becoming almost indecipherable. She paused a moment, grabbed a couple of tissues from the box on the table, wiped her eyes, sighed and continued.

"I had no idea what to do after high school. I was so terrified that when I spoke to the counselor and she asked me what I liked to do, I couldn't think of anything. So I told her about all the things you liked--children, teaching, learning. She told me I should become a teacher. You were doing it and you seemed so happy about it, so I thought it would make me happy too," a new wave of tears and a few sobs escaped Chrissy, and she grabbed more tissues.

"I don't like teaching at all," Chrissy said finally, and the admission seemed to bring her enormous relief. She looked up at Elnora and concern came into her eyes. "I love children," she said earnestly, "Really, I do. But teaching is just too hard. There are so many things going on at once, and you have to juggle so many balls in the air. Plus, some of the parents are so very difficult to work with," she paused, and Elnora nodded in agreement. "I just don't like teaching. It's not for me."

Elnora smiled gently at her friend. "Then don't do it," she said, simply, and shrugged. Chrissy's face took on a look of surprise. "The counselor was right. You should do something you enjoy. *You*. I had no idea you did all those things because of me. I'm flattered, but I wouldn't have been offended if you had never done a single thing I had done. Our friendship has deeper roots and commonality to be hurt by that," she rubbed Chrissy's back. "But if you don't like teaching, and especially if it causes anxiety and stress, then you really need to stop. Now. Find out what you like, what makes you happy, what calms your nerves," she said with feeling, leaning forward and looking into her friend's red-rimmed eyes, "And do that."

"I honestly don't know what that is," Chrissy said, her voice calm.

"Then you need to go find out," Elnora suggested, and Chrissy nodded.

"But what about ..." Chrissy stopped before completing her sentence and just waved toward the spare bedroom.

Elnora nodded. "You'll need to handle that. I'm not going to tell you how, but you'll need to handle that. And you'll need to stop. Get whatever help you need to handle your anxiety--whether by talking to someone who understands you and can make you feel better," she paused pointedly and waited for Chrissy to look at her, "Or by talking walks, doing yoga, getting massages, eating dark chocolate--whatever it is that works for you." Elnora paused again. "Chrissy, it's okay to need help and it's definitely okay to ask for it. But you *have* to ask for it. And you definitely need to stop doing things that make it worse."

"What do you think they'll do?" Chrissy asked.

"Who?" Elnora asked.

"The school," Chrissy said. "I mean, when I leave. What do you think they'll do?"

Elnora looked at her friend, and saw the nervousness in her eyes. "I don't know, but I'm positive they'll handle it. Don't worry about that. Focus on you for a change."

Chrissy nodded and relaxed, smiling a little. "I'm sorry," she said, sincerely. Elnora looked over at her, and Chrissy met her eyes. "For putting you through this. I'm sorry," she repeated.

Elnora patted her arm. "It's okay, you haven't put me through anything. I'm sorry you've been struggling with this for so long. But you can set it to rights and move forward, and that's what's most important."

They sat quietly together for a few minutes longer and then began to talk again, this time about Elnora's developing relationship with Kevin. Chrissy seemed to know anyway, and Elnora felt it was appropriate to do whatever she could to help lighten her friend's mood. Her own feelings were in complete turmoil, but she was certain she was effectively hiding this from her friend. Being an incredibly honest person herself, she found it difficult to not demand instant restoration of the "borrowed" items. On the other hand, she now understood how important it was to support her friend in getting the help she needed, not in pressing her to do things that would surely bring her greater discomfort.

The sky grew dimmer outside the windows and they both recognized that it was time for dinner. Chrissy's eyes dimmed with panic--clearly she believed that Elnora would be leaving soon for home. Elnora reached over and rubbed her friend's back.

"Want to join me and Kevin for dinner?"

Chrissy's face lit up, and then fell. "No," she said. "I mean, I want to, but I also don't want to interrupt."

"You're not interrupting. And I'm not leaving you alone right now. *And* you have to eat. So come on, get ready--we're going to the inn restaurant."

Chrissy smiled gratefully at her friend and then hurried to the bathroom to wash her face and brush her hair. She returned a few moments later, looking a little tired but much better, and nodded at her friend. Elnora grabbed Chrissy's keys from the hook beside the door, pulled the door shut behind them and locked the door. Chrissy walked to the passenger side door of her own car, silently agreeing that Elnora should drive. Elnora slid into the driver's side, started the car, backed it out of the driveway and drove slowly through town to the inn.

The parking space closest to the front door of the restaurant was vacant, and Elnora pulled into it, shutting off the car and opening the door. She and Chrissy went inside and got a booth near the back, but Elnora didn't sit down.

"We're a little later than we had planned to meet, so Kevin isn't here anymore," Elnora explained. Chrissy looked upset. "It's okay," Elnora assured her friend. "He's very kind and he'll definitely understand--without my explaining everything. I'm just going to go collect him, and we'll have a nice dinner." Chrissy nodded and reached for the menu.

Elnora stepped out the front door of the restaurant and glanced down at her watch. It was 6:15--she was very late. She cut through the parking lot to the inn office, and as she got closer she recognized Ricky Hunter sitting at the counter. She smiled, opening the door into the lobby.

"Hi Ricky," she said lightly.

Ricky looked up from the magazine he was reading and smiled at Elnora. He was sixteen years old, with the acne-mottled face that often came with that age. His long blonde hair hung forward into his face, and he swung it out of his eyes. "Hi Elnora. What can I do for you?"

"I know Kevin Hiller is staying here," Elnora began, and Ricky raised his eyebrows. "We were supposed to meet for dinner and I am running a little late. Can you tell me which room he's in so I can apologize properly?"

Ricky shrugged his shoulders. "I'm not really supposed to give out room numbers," he said.

"I know," Elnora said, smiling her gentle smile.

"But I guess it's okay if you just want to apologize," Ricky said. "He's in room 32."

"Thank you, Ricky," Elnora said, turning and walking out of the lobby.

Kevin's old car was parked almost directly in front of his room. Elnora paused in front of the door, her heart pounding in her chest, and then rapped lightly with her knuckles. Kevin opened the door mere seconds later, and smiled at her.

"You're late," he said, teasing her.

"I know, I'm so sorry," Elnora said. "I got stuck at Chrissy's house, helping her with something. Time ran a bit away from me."

"Boy, I'll say," Kevin teased again.

"Are you still up for dinner?" Elnora asked. "I'll treat, to show you just how sorry I am."

Kevin smiled widely, the boyish grin that Elnora was already a bit enamored of. "Now you know that's not going to happen," he said. "I'm a gentleman, after all." He flipped off the light and stepped out beside her, pulling the door closed behind him.

"I brought Chrissy with me," Elnora said as soon as Kevin stepped away from the door. "She needs company--and distraction," she explained.

Kevin nodded. “I’ll be happy to provide both,” he said, taking Elnora’s hand.

They walked together to the restaurant, joined Chrissy in the booth, and together the three of them pleasantly passed the next several hours chatting, eating and chatting some more. For Elnora, it would’ve been absolutely perfect, if not for the fact that in the back of her mind, she knew it was probably one of the last times she would be hanging out with her friend like this before things changed.

Long after their food had been eaten and their plates had been cleared, Chrissy excused herself to the restroom. Kevin took advantage of her absence and leaned forward, his voice low.

“I’m sorry about Chrissy,” he said.

Elnora responded immediately with a look of surprise. “What?” escaped her mouth before she had even had a chance to think about it.

“Well you explained that you were late because you got caught up at her house, helping with something,” Kevin explained, “And there’s a tinge of sadness in your voice when you talk to her. I can only assume that she’s going through a difficult time.”

Elnora nodded and then felt the sudden, burning sensation of tears forming in her eyes. “She is,” she admitted, using her cloth napkin to wipe her eyes.

“Is it going to be okay?” Kevin asked, and then added, “I mean, do you need help in order to help her?”

“I really don’t know,” Elnora said honestly. “It’s up to Chrissy. But I think she will be okay. This meant a lot to her, I know. She needs friends right now.”

Kevin smiled, reached out and placed his hand over hers. “You’re a good friend,” he said, and Elnora looked up into his soft brown eyes. “She’s very lucky to have you.”

Elnora smiled shakily, revealing the pain she felt for her friend. "Thank you," she said.

Kevin asked nothing further and Elnora was grateful. She wasn't sure she would be able to keep secrets from him if directly asked, but on the other hand her loyalty to her friend and her desire to protect her ran deep. She felt a new surge of affinity for the man sitting across from her, and she couldn't stop the easy smile that broke out across her face.

Chrissy returned from the restroom, and though they all tried to get a conversation started up again, it was clear they were all tired and ready to go home to bed. Finally, they sighed collectively, looked at each other, and pushed sideways out of the booth to stand. Kevin had long since paid their bill, over Elnora's and Chrissy's protests, and the hostess nodded at them as they walked out to the parking lot. They walked quietly to Chrissy's car and Elnora unlocked it so Chrissy could get in.

"I'm just going to walk Kevin back to his room, okay?" Elnora asked her friend, and Chrissy nodded.

Kevin and Elnora turned and walked quietly back to the door of his room, then stood there for a few minutes like awkward teenagers, not wanting the evening to end. Kevin reached out and took Elnora's hand, pulling her gently to him. They kissed, Elnora's stomach once again filled with butterflies, and when they pulled away they were both smiling.

"Until tomorrow?" Kevin asked and Elnora nodded. He winked at her and then turned, walking away toward his room. Elnora returned to Chrissy's car, got in, started it up, and backed out of the parking spot.

"You guys really like each other, don't you?" Chrissy asked, her voice absent of any sort of teasing tone.

"Yeah," Elnora said simply. She turned her head and

caught the back of Kevin just as he stepped into his room. She smiled and put the car into drive, pulling forward slowly and heading back to Chrissy's house.

Elnora opened Chrissy's front door and the two friends stumbled through it exhaustedly. Chrissy gathered some blankets and a spare pillow and brought them into the living room, where Elnora worked to turn the couch into a bed. They both knew that Chrissy shouldn't be alone that night and that she had a challenging few weeks ahead of her. After Elnora had made her bed and taken a seat on it, Chrissy sat down on the coffee table across from her.

"Thank you," Chrissy said, looking carefully at her friend. Elnora nodded, reached out for her friend, and gave her another hug. Chrissy padded quietly away to her bedroom, shutting off the lights as she went and leaving Elnora in darkness.

Elnora lay down on her makeshift bed, turning to face the kitchen. In the dim light filtering through the kitchen windows, she could see the beautiful glass jellyfish, dangling from the darkened kitchen light. She closed her eyes, and fell asleep.

CHAPTER 39

BLUE WHALE COVE, OR -- Many Blue Whale Cove residents are rejoicing over the return of personal items that, in some cases, have been missing for over a decade.

"I thought I'd lost my great-grandmother's ruby ring forever," one resident said. "It's wonderful to have it back!"

"I've been searching for my antique glass Christmas ornaments for longer than I can remember. I'm so relieved to have them restored to me!" another resident said.

The return of the lost treasures is, itself, an unsolved mystery. Blue Whale Cove Chief of Police, Douglas Hinson, reports that they were contained in several unmarked canvas bags that had been deposited in front of the police station's rear entrance early Wednesday morning last week. Most of the items, being delicate in nature, were carefully wrapped in many layers of tissue paper and bubble wrap.

When asked whether the individual who returned the items had been identified on one of the station's many surveillance cameras, Chief Hinson shook his head.

"It would appear that the individual knew the precise placement and angle of the cameras--he remained out of sight until the final seconds, at which point all that was seen was essentially a large, black shadow depositing the bags at the rear entrance.

"There is no indication of who had the items, how they acquired them, or why they have returned them," Chief Hinson told the Journal. "However, I can confirm that some of the items had been reported as burgled."

Chief Hinson is referring to the series of burglaries that occurred in Blue Whale Cove between March 4th and March 13th, after which many residents chose to report their missing items as burglaries.

"With the absence of reported burglaries over the past month, and the apparent return of other missing and burgled items, we are assuming that the individual or individuals responsible have decided to atone for their actions," Chief Hinson stated. "We will remain vigilant, but we are hopeful that this small crime wave is now over."

CHAPTER 40

It was 7:00 am on Saturday, April 28th, and Elnora was busily vacuuming her house. More than a month had passed since her rather surprising afternoon with Chrissy, and much had changed. Chrissy had given her two-week notice at the school the very next day, and after successfully renting out her house (she wasn't entirely sure yet if she wanted to sell it), she had moved down to live in Ashland, Oregon with her parents.

Elnora missed her friend, but they talked on the phone almost every day and Chrissy sounded happy and calm. She told Elnora that she was currently working at a pet shop and exploring a possible career in dog training. It was challenging, but it was a level of challenge that she felt confident she could easily handle. More importantly, she was pursuing it because she was truly interested in it, not because anyone else was doing it. Chrissy assured her friend that she hadn't "borrowed" anything since "that day" and honestly wasn't even fighting the urge to do so.

Elnora and Kevin had continued to grow their relationship, and they often spent some time each day in one another's company. They had spoken briefly of the future--a future together, and Elnora was amazed at how easy that was to imagine. She loved being around him, no matter the occasion. In fact, she was joining him at Anna's office at 10:00 am when he would finally sign the closing papers for his Aunt Sam's house.

The small, safe town of Blue Whale Cove, where everyone seemed to know everyone else, had slipped back into a wonderful rhythm of innocence--the very sort that the residents preferred.

EPILOGUE

On Sunday, April 29th, at 5:00 am, Julie Irskin, a second-generation Blue Whale Cove resident, put on her sweatsuit, grabbed a clean towel, and walked out of her bedroom, down the short hallway to her living room, into her kitchen, where she grabbed her sports bottle, and out the door into her garage.

Julie turned on the garage light, set her towel and bottle on the chair that was placed against the wall and then turned on first the large television mounted to the wall and then her exercise bike. Using the remote control, Julie selected a pre-recorded episode of *House Hunters* that she had not yet seen, turned the volume up high, and then set down the remote, and got onto her exercise bike.

Half an hour later, Julie got off her exercise bike, turned off the bike and the television, grabbed her towel, wiped her face and picked up her sports bottle. She took a long drink of the cool water, shut off the garage light, and stepped back into her house.

Julie set the sports bottle on the kitchen counter and moved into her living room, pulling her towel back up to wipe her face and neck. "Ow!" she exclaimed as her elbow hit the open door of her glass curio cabinet. Julie stopped and stared at the cabinet in confusion. "Why is the door …?" she began, and then stopped.

On the middle shelf, in between two beautifully-detailed resin teddy bears, where Julie had proudly displayed her grandmother's delicate Waterford crystal vase, there was now only empty space.